# midnight sun

# midnight sun

## Trish Cook

POPPY
LITTLE, BROWN AND COMPANY
New York  Boston

Little, Brown and Company
Hachette Book Group
1290 Avenue of the Americas, New York, NY 10104
Visit us at LBYR.com

First Edition: February 2018

Little, Brown and Company is a division of Hachette Book Group, Inc.
The Little, Brown name and logo are trademarks of Hachette Book Group, Inc.

The publisher is not responsible for websites (or their content) that are not owned by the publisher.

Library of Congress Control Number: 2017933410

ISBNs: 978-0-316-47357-6 (paperback), 978-0-316-47356-9 (ebook)

Printed in the United States of America

LSC-C

10 9 8

# midnight sun

# 1

I have this recurring dream: I'm a little girl, sitting with my mom, and she's singing to me. We're at the beach on an old blanket I still have tucked away in my closet. I hear the waves crashing as my mom's voice rises and falls. I feel the warmth of the sun on my skin and the comfort of her arms around me.

I want to stay in this moment forever.

When I wake up, I miss the dream. I miss the sun. I miss my mom.

I want so badly for this dream to be real, but that would be impossible because my mom died when I was six years old.

And I can't go out into the sun...like, at all. I have a rare genetic condition called xeroderma pigmentosum, aka XP, which basically means a severe sensitivity to sunlight. If sunlight so much as glances off my skin, I'll get skin cancer, and my body can't repair the damage so my brain starts to fail—which could mean hearing loss, difficulty walking and swallowing, movement problems, loss of intellectual function and capacity for speech, seizures, and, oh yeah, death.

Pretty fun, right?

So I spend my days indoors, hanging out with my dad (truly the best dad ever) and Morgan (truly the best friend ever).

Morgan and I used to pretend that I was like Rapunzel from *Tangled*, hidden away in my darkened tower (bedroom). We watched that movie about a hundred times when it came out. Rapunzel finally went stir-crazy and broke out of there with some dude. Now that I'm older, I completely and totally relate, girl.

I guess if there's one other thing I have in common

with Rapunzel, it's that I'm going to have to keep the faith and keep on fighting until I get my happily ever after. Mine might not be destined to last as long as other people's—but that doesn't mean it will be any less awesome.

# 2

**There I go, rambling again.** It's a habit that gets me in trouble sometimes. You'll see. For now, let me back up and start from the beginning.

Hi! I'm Katie Price, and I guess from the outside looking in—if you could actually see in my windows, which you can't, thanks to the solar shades that block every bit of UV light from getting in my house—you might think I'm some pathetic sick girl who's always staring out the window watching life go by. But I'm actually just like everyone else, with the major exception of the "can't go out in the sun" thing.

I play guitar and write lyrics and poetry and think I sound awesome when I sing in the shower. I love astronomy and hope to be an astrophysicist someday. I hate brussels sprouts, love Chinese food, think pugs are the most adorable dogs on the planet, and get freaked out by spiders. My best friend—let's face it, my only IRL friend other than my dad (okay, that right there just made me sound truly sad, right?)—Morgan, kicks butt and would for sure kick your butt if you don't agree.

And, oh yeah, I just so happen to have an enormous crush on a guy named Charlie Reed. Ever since I got banished to this house during daylight hours by my XP diagnosis in first grade, I've watched him pass by my window on his way to school. Over time, watching Charlie go by became a part of my routine. Along with constant doctor appointments, sleeping during the day and staying up all night—which from what I hear is the dream schedule of most kids my age—and playing music. During the week, he's the last person I see every morning before I go to sleep and the first person I see every afternoon when I wake up. While I'm getting my "night's" sleep, he goes off to school and swim practice. He's living his normal, perfect life. He's basically grown up right in front of my eyes and gotten cuter with every year. He's a senior now, tall and lanky with gorgeous floppy hair and eyes that could melt an iceberg faster than global warming. The only thing standing in the way of our great love affair is...he has no idea I even exist.

When he dragged our trash can out of the street after a windy night—after literally everyone else just walked by it—he didn't know I was watching. When he stopped to help Mrs. Graham from across the street with her groceries. I've seen the thoughtful little things he does, even when he thinks no one is around to notice.

It's not like I can just walk out my door one morning and casually bump into him on the street because then I'd fry to death. (Don't worry—it wouldn't happen that fast. But, trust me, it wouldn't be pretty.) I would be lying if I said I didn't fantasize about one day making a grand gesture, though. Like, I don't know, bang on the window when I see him. Wave him into the house (when my dad's not looking, I guess). Invite him upstairs. (Where my dad won't follow us? Ha! Let me dream.) Run my fingers through that gorgeous hair. Kiss him.

Fine. Not going to happen. I know.

I'll just watch him like I always have (in a totally

noncreepy way!)—at least until that unfortunately placed tree blocks my view—and wish him well on the stars when they come out tonight. Wish that he's happy to be graduating high school today and that he's headed for a life full of excitement and adventure. That he gets everything he ever dreamed of. He deserves it. We all do. My biggest wish (to have a normal life—trying not to be bitter here) will never come true, but I sure hope Charlie's does.

I open my laptop to watch the live stream of what would have been my graduation, too. That is, if I hadn't been homeschooled since first grade. It's a little anticlimactic for me, seeing as I've already accumulated enough online credits to be a college sophomore at this point. What can I say? I like learning. Plus, I've got a lot more time on my hands than most kids.

Still, it's graduation. A defining moment in most people's lives. Not sure it symbolizes anything more than the same old same old in my case, though. Come the fall, I'll still be sitting here in my room, taking classes online, endlessly avoiding the sun instead of heading off to some fabulous university. Sigh. Somehow I'm feeling nostalgic nonetheless.

Names are called, and kids stream onstage to shake

the principal's hand. They leave clutching a newly minted diploma. Morgan heads for the camera instead of the stairs after getting hers, then strikes a pose and mouths, *Yeah, bitches!* She's quickly redirected back into line, but not before I laugh so hard I snort. I wasn't sure she'd actually go through with it—but when have I ever known Morgan to back down from one of my dares?

I impatiently wait for them to get to the *R*s. Wow, there are a lot of *P*s in this class (minus this one, of course). And a *Q*? What are the odds? (Ooh, poor girl. I assume Quackenbush was not a high-school-friendly last name.) They're finally calling Charlie's name. I can't wait to see how dignified and handsome he looks in his graduation gown, how melty fabulous those eyes are under his cap. Just as Charlie steps into the frame, my dad bursts into my room.

"Katie Price!" he booms.

He's standing there with a goofy grin on his face and a rolled-up piece of paper in his hand. At this point, most girls would probably yell something like "UGH! Would you PLEASE get out of here." But I know he's only trying to make me happy and feel included, so I close my laptop and laugh instead. He has, of course, put in the extra effort; why not let him feel good about it? It's not his fault I'm sitting on my bed right now instead of walking across that stage with the rest of my class.

Wait, I take that back. It kind of *is* his fault. Make that half his fault and half my mom's. Both needed to contribute a mutated recessive gene to give me XP. Whatever. He didn't mean to, obviously.

"What are you wearing?"

"The faculty and staff always wear a cap and gown, and so do the students," he replies, holding out the hat part of the getup.

I take it from him and put it on. He hands me the hand-printed diploma that states I am now an official homeschooled high school graduate. There's a little footnote that acknowledges I already have twenty-four college credits to my name. I smile up at my dad and shake his hand. Mostly, and especially at times like this, I like how well he knows me. He understands how much value I place on my academic accomplishments, since learning is one of the few things in life the sun can't screw up for me. Dad understands I'd rather stand out for my brains than for inheriting a disease that affects only one in a million.

"So, as valedictorian, I assume you have a speech prepared?" he asks.

I adjust my cap and think about what I can say to

commemorate this really-not-all-that-special day. "Well, I would definitely like to offer a great thanks to my head-master," I begin.

"Ah, well, you're welcome," my dad says, his eyes twin-kling.

"And my Spanish teacher—"

*"De nada."* He tips an imaginary hat.

"And my English teacher—"

My dad gives a little bow here. "It was my pleasure!"

"And state again for the record that my gym teacher had no idea what he was doing."

Dad throws a hand over his heart. "Oh, that's a low blow," he exclaims. "I was going to give you this card, but now..."

He dangles it close to me, then snatches it back when I try to grab it. I shrug like I don't care. He admits defeat and drops it gently in my lap, then plops himself down on the edge of my bed.

I reach into the oversize envelope and pull out a card. It is cartoony and corny, and features a smiling star wearing a graduation cap. Emblazoned across the front in cheese-ball Comic Sans font it says: *ConGRADuation, Superstar!*

I roll my eyes. "This is the dorkiest card I've ever seen."

"I know," he says with a grave nod. "I went to three stores to find a card that lame. All right, are you ready for your present?"

"Present?" I wasn't expecting a gift. "What present?"

My dad jumps up and hustles out into the hallway. He comes back a few seconds later carrying a weathered guitar case with a single red bow on it.

I already know that inside is the most gorgeous instrument I've ever seen, with a cool tortoise-colored sunburst body and inlaid mother-of-pearl frets. I pick it up gently and run my hand along its smooth surface until a tiny set of grooves stops me. I look down at the spot where my fingers have come to rest and see the initials TJP. My mom's initials.

I look up at my dad, and before I can say thank you, he says, "You've outgrown that kids' guitar," gesturing to the one in the corner of my room. "But I know this one is old, so if you want a newer one—"

I shake my head to cut him off before he can even finish the crazy thought. Having Mom's guitar is like having a small part of her with me always. The thought fills a tiny bit of the gaping hole in my heart she left behind, the one that will never fully heal. "I love it. So much."

I stand up to hug him. He hugs me back, holding on tightly. We're probably both about to burst into tears. I let go to try to regroup. Awkward silence ensues.

"All right, well...try to get some sleep," he finally says, giving me a kiss on the head. "I'm proud of you, Peanut."

No need to feel sorry for me about my life of sleeping during the day. It's probably the most normal thing about me. I know this for a fact because there are tons of people—including kids my age—online all night, every night, and it's definitely not because they're forced to live an upside-down life like mine.

I've found a couple of online communities for people with rare diseases, and even though I'll never meet any of these people in real life and we all have different symptoms and are at different stages in our diseases, it's nice to know they're out there.

The Internet is full of info about XP. I learned about a small village in Brazil where one in forty people have XP, which is insane for a condition that usually affects only one in a million. And in the Navajo population, it affects one in thirty thousand. What's that about?

And I've followed chains of people off of Morgan's social media—some of them people I used to know. It's shockingly easy to spend an hour going down the rabbit hole of a stranger's life. I stalk their Facebook statuses and Snapchats and Instagrams and blogs, watching how easily they navigate the world with undisguised FOMO. I consider trying to make friends with the ones I seem to have the most in common with; I type comments and the perfect replies to their captions. But I never actually end up posting anything or DMing anyone to try to forge a new relationship. Because how disappointing and awkward would it be if the person I reached out to reacted to my XP the same way the kids I used to go to school with back at Purdue Elementary did?

Zoe Carmichael had been the absolute worst. It's not like we'd ever been friends, but we weren't enemies. When I got diagnosed after a school trip to the beach that ended with me in the emergency room because my skin burned so badly, she started a rumor that I was a vampire, and that was that. Everyone was terrified of me, they started calling me Vampire Girl, and no one but Morgan would even talk to me anymore. Charlie had just moved to town and joined our class that year. We'd never talked (because back then I was all, *Eww, boys*), but I remember that when some of his friends were making fun of me he told them to stop and smiled at me apologetically. That was my last day at school. After that, my dad homeschooled me. And we started getting ice cream and going to the movies in other nearby towns just so I wouldn't have to endure kids like Zoe (or actual Zoe) staring and pointing at me whenever we ventured out at night.

And that's pretty much why I figure it's better to stick to who and what I know than take a chance trying to branch out friendship-wise in the real world. I refuse to give any more bullies an invitation into my life.

# 3

I wake up from my "night's" sleep to a ruckus outside my window: car horns blaring, kids whooping, general celebrating. This part I know I could participate in—if only Morgan actually liked anyone in our graduating class. Which she doesn't. And if Morgan isn't going to whatever parties might be happening right now, that means I'm not going either.

## HOW I IMAGINE A SCHOOL PARTY WITHOUT MORGAN WOULD GO

Zoe Carmichael (who Morgan says is still a total mean girl): Who *are* you?

Me: I ... um ...

Zoe's Minion: Are you even in our class?

Me: Well, you see, I kind of had to study from home ... extenuating circumstances ... but I would have graduated from Purdue High today otherwise ...

Zoe (studying me carefully): Oh wait, no, I remember. You're Vampire Girl, right?

Zoe's Minion (screaming her head off): *Aaaaah.*


*The whole party goes silent. Everyone clutches their necks to keep from being bitten by me. I slink home and drown my sorrows in takeout Chinese food with my dad.*


And ... scene.

So there's no way I can go without Morgan. And she's stubborn as anything about not "fraternizing with the snotty girls and fratty boys in the popular crowd at PHS, especially that flaming crotch rot Zoe Carmichael."

Even though it's not like I think we'd have the best time ever if we were celebrating with our class tonight, we could probably avoid Zoe and her crew, and hang with the nice people instead. There have to be at least a few, right?

There's a song by an Australian singer-songwriter named Courtney Barnett that I feel like sums up my entire existence as it pertains to parties: "I wanna go out but I wanna stay home."

## HOW I IMAGINE A SCHOOL PARTY *WITH* MORGAN WOULD GO

Zoe: Who *are* you?

Me: I … um …

Morgan: She's my best friend, and she's hotter
    than you'll ever be.

Zoe's Minion: Are you even in our class?

Me: Well, you see, I kind of had—

Morgan (covering my mouth with her hand
    before I can say anything else): You ditched
    so many classes you barely graduated. Who
    are you to talk?

Zoe (studying me carefully): Oh wait, no, I
    remember. You're Vampire Girl, right?

Morgan (before I can even try to defend
        myself): That's right. Say anything more
        and she makes you undead forever.


    *We go play beer pong and I officially meet
    Charlie Reed and we fall madly in love and my
    dad never finds out I went to a party instead of
    going to Morgan's to watch Netflix like I said I
    was.*


I sigh and throw the covers off my bed. My eyes land
on my new guitar, and I decide to head to the train station
to try it out. By myself. Just me, myself, and I. If I can get
my dad to agree to my plan, that is.

I hope he realizes how much I need my independence
right now. Years of hanging with my father in places kids
usually hit with friends—the movies, the mall, the bowling
alley, the fro-yo joint—doesn't do much to dispel the impression that having XP somehow makes me a superweird person. I know Dad does everything in his power to give me a
normal life and I appreciate it, but his efforts don't change
the fact that the way I have to live is not now and will never
be normal. Like when he watches a different movie in the
same theater complex so I won't be the loser girl who went

out with her dad on a Saturday night? Not normal either. Because who goes to the movies alone on a Saturday night? Right. No one but a superweird loser—and me. Which people generally would assume are one and the same.

Tonight I just want to be Katie the normal girl who doesn't have a rare disease and whose father doesn't follow her around nervously all the time.

I toss my hair into a messy bun, grab the case, and head downstairs. I look for my dad in the den. He's not there. I try the kitchen next; maybe he's having a snack. Nope. There's only one place left. I go to the basement and see the telltale glow coming from underneath the darkroom door. I knock.

"Come on in!" Dad calls from inside.

When I open the door, I'm hit by how bittersweet the vibe is in here. The walls are plastered with magazine covers he shot in exotic locales. There's an impoverished village in India. An arctic glacier rising out of a churning gray sea. A tranquil savannah in Africa punctuated by a lone giraffe. Glimpses of a life that once was and isn't anymore. It makes me proud of all the things my dad used to do and be, and sad he doesn't go anywhere anymore because of my "condition." Proud that my dad is so talented, and sad he's wasting it on this nothing town.

He's got a bunch of newer shots hanging from a

clothesline. In addition to a few landscapes, there are a ton of me. Candid pictures, ones he badgered me into posing for, and now the latest from earlier today: me playing Mom's guitar. Most of the other ones embarrass me, but I kind of like how I look there.

"That's a good one," I say.

He points at me hovering above the gorgeous guitar. "That part is kinda weird, though."

I playfully punch him in the arm. He laughs and dodges away. I'm grateful for his relaxed mood; it'll be easier to convince him to let me go out alone tonight. It's not that I mind that he always finds an excuse to tag along. But how will I ever get honest feedback about my songs with my daddy standing right there next to me?

"Any schmuck can take a good photo of such a beautiful subject," he says.

I roll my eyes and walk over to one of my favorite photos of his, a group of Pakistani girls in school uniforms outside a worn-down building. "Now *this* is a beautiful subject," I say, turning to face him. "How can you not miss it?"

"All that travel?" My dad scoffs. "It was miserable."

He moves elegantly through the room. He makes taking and developing great photos look easy. But I know better. He didn't become one of the most highly sought-after photojournalists in the world by being a hack. He notices my expression, the one that says, *Come on, now. You can't expect me to believe that.*

"I'm serious," he insists, nodding at the photo I'm standing in front of. "That trip, somebody stole my bags and I ended up wearing the same clothes for a week. I had to sleep on my guide's floor, no mattress, no blanket. It was so cold I just lay there all night waiting for the sun to rise."

He's full of it. Of course he misses that life. Who wouldn't? I'd give anything to be able to go anywhere in the world anytime I wanted to and see everything I'll probably never get to see.

"I'd much rather sleep in my own bed and teach younger knuckleheads how to go out and get dirty," he concludes.

"You're a terrible liar," I tell him.

He gives me a look, like he's about to divulge something more than the always happy, always positive front he always puts on for me, but then he seems to think better of it. Nothing to be gained from opening that particular can of worms, I guess, but for once I'd love to have an open, honest conversation about how XP has changed just about everything in our lives. I'm the reason he can't follow his dreams anymore, and we both know it.

"So what's up?" he asks instead.

I take a deep breath and then let forth a fast stream of words. I figure that way he has less of a chance to get a word in edgewise, which translates to less of a chance of his saying no. "I was wondering if I could go play my new graduation present at the train station tonight?"

It comes out like this: *IwaswonderingifIcouldgoplaymy newgraduationpresentatthetrainstationtonight?*

I add a huge smile at the end, meant to convey: *I am a competent, confident high school graduate now (with twenty-four college credits!). I am fully capable of walking half a mile down the road and playing my guitar for any late-night commuters who happen to be around. Which will probably be no one, but still. I already checked, and Fred, the station manager, will be there, and you guys have known each other since you were a kid so I will be safe, I promise. PLEASE DON'T SUGGEST COMING WITH ME.*

My dad's face falls like a ruined soufflé, and he taps his watch. I honestly don't know what kind of horrible outcome he's imagining might befall me if I venture outside without him—probably we've watched way too many horror movies over the years and his mind is in overdrive—

but our sleepy little town has, like, a zero percent crime rate. I'll be fine. I know he doesn't want to agree, but he can't quite come up with a good reason to deny my request yet. So he's stalling. "It's already ten o'clock. Why can't Morgan come over? Or you could just play for me here."

While playing for my biggest fan is nice—whatever I've performed is always THE BEST THING HE'S EVER HEARD or THAT ONE IS GOING STRAIGHT TO NUMBER ONE—I feel like I not only have to play for more than one person to get better, but I also have to play for people who are the teensiest bit less biased toward thinking I'm the next Taylor Swift only much, much better.

TBH, I just want to escape this house for a while, and my dad, too. The cabin fever I have to fight on the daily is in full force at the moment.

"She's busy with her family," I tell him, using my sweetest voice possible. XP has taught me a lot of patience. I know better than to try to shove what I want down my dad's throat. That kind of tactic never works with him; logical, well-crafted arguments do. "And I love playing for you, but I need to expand my audience. My fan page has exactly three likes right now—you, Dr. Fleming, and Morgan. I've got to do a better job of putting myself out there. And I graduated today; isn't it the American tradition to extend my curfew?"

He's silent. Still unconvinced. At best, he's probably about to grab his keys and say he'll drive me there and *Oh, while I'm here, let me just hear one song*, which will then turn into my entire set.

I need to turn this thing around. "Fred will be there, and he'll look out for me. Plus, I have this amazing new guitar case designed to be left open to catch quarters and dollar bills, which I know you wouldn't have given me if you yourself didn't want me to go play..."

My dad frowns. I know he wants to protect me. Make that *overprotect* me. But I hate being treated like a fragile creature who just might drop dead every time she leaves the house.

"I will extend your curfew for *one* hour. Which means midnight—"

"THANK YOU!" I squeal before he can change his mind. "Thank you, thank you, you're the best dad in the world, thank you—"

Now come the qualifiers, but I'm used to this sort of thing. I nod my head gravely as he sets the rules for my solo pass out into the world even though I'm not really listening. I don't need to. He says the same thing every time.

"Text me every hour, or I won't just call Fred; I'll actually come down there, and it'll be so embarrassing it will become an urban legend about why kids should stick to their curfew."

I grab my guitar and head for the door before he can inject a tracking device into my arm.

"Every hour, Katie," he reminds me before I can escape.

I give him a big grin over my shoulder as I'm leaving. "Love you!"

I step outside. Cool night air fills my lungs. It has been two days (well, nights) since I've ventured past the front porch. I exhale and stare up at the stars. They wink back at me, like they think something magical is about to happen.

My dad stands in the doorway watching me. "Love you more."

"Not possible!" I tell him, and head off.

# 4

Fred is where I always find him, sitting in his little office at the train station ticket window. He's one of dad's oldest buddies, both in the amount of time they've known each other and also in chronological age. They were neighbors back in the day, when Fred was Dad's some-time babysitter. He has great stories about what a little pain in the ass my dad was as a kid.

I wave to Fred to get his attention. "Hey-o, Fred."

He looks up, his mop of silver hair gleaming in the

moonlight. "The graduate! I was wondering if you were gonna show up tonight."

I gesture around at the empty platform. "And disappoint all my fans?"

Fred laughs appreciatively even though this has been our running joke for the past few years. Then he spies my awesome old-new instrument, which is most definitely different than the one I normally have with me. His expressive face registers so much delight and surprise that he basically morphs into a real-live heart-eyed emoji.

"Is that a new guitar?"

I pat it proudly and nod. "It was my mom's," I tell him, and his eyes soften. Then I turn to find my spot. After a last wish upon the brightest star out tonight that something truly exciting will happen for once, I open my guitar case.

I launch into one of my newest compositions—a song called "Waiting for the Sun"—as two tired and dazed-looking people step off the train. The melody is slow and deep, and pretty much matches their pace. The first guy seems drunk, and he almost falls on top of me before stumbling around the spot where I'm playing. The other is a lady in a severe red pantsuit who is definitely not drunk. She walks past me without even making eye contact.

And then no one for a good half an hour. I keep playing and singing like I'm headlining at Carnegie Hall. Finally, another train rumbles into the station. A girl I suspect may be one of Zoe's many minions gets off, eyes me curiously, and then drops a half-eaten bag of Skittles into the case.

"Thanks a lot," I call after her as she walks away.

She looks back over her shoulder and gives me a little shrug and a lot more attitude. Whatever. I'm no quitter. I launch into another original.

A thirtysomething hipster-looking guy with a lumberjack beard appears at the top of the stairs and donates a few coins to my case. It's not even enough to feed the parking meter, so good thing I walked here. Dad doesn't think I'm "ready" for my license yet. I wonder if he's afraid I'd just drive off into the sunset if I had a way to. Who knows, maybe I *would* pull a Rapunzel. But I don't really have anywhere to go, so I don't bother fighting him on that one.

Just when I think it's going to be a totally typical slow night, an angel-faced little boy tugs on his mom's hand, making the two of them stop short right in front of me. It's clear the kid should be home in bed, but he seems entranced by my song. He's completely digging it and will not move until I finish. Then he claps his little hands off.

"What's your name?" I ask as the applause fades into silence. Too bad he's too young to be on Facebook, or I'm pretty sure I'd have my fourth official like on my fan page.

"Tommy," he says. "I'm taking the night train."

"That's very cool," I tell him.

He makes his hands into chubby little fists and sticks them on his hips. "Are you taking a train?"

I shake my head and smile. "Nope. I'm just playing here."

"Why are you playing so late?" he asks. And I have to admit, it's a valid question. There'd be way more people to ignore me and give me half-eaten bags of Skittles during morning rush hour. Smart kid, this one. I decide to give it to him straight.

"Because I can't go out in the sun."

He squints at me, assessing things. He quickly comes to the same conclusion all the other kids did when I was his age. "So you're a vampire?"

I laugh. It would probably be easier being a vampire because my life expectancy would be centuries longer and

I wouldn't feel such pressure to do something huge and earth-shattering just to prove I was here for the limited time I have. "I wish. That'd be much cooler. But it's more like a really bad allergy."

He nods. "I'm allergic to strawberries. My nose gets runny and I get hives."

"That sucks," I tell him, glancing up at his mom. I hope she's not mad about my mildly bad language. But she's staring at her phone, fingers flying all over the keyboard. I'm in the clear; I don't think she even heard me.

"What happens to you if you're in the sun?" Tommy asks.

I scrunch up my face and shrug. I certainly don't want to scare the kid by telling him I'd be complete toast if I went out in it for too long. Or give him a lecture on the ugly realities of skin cancer. I finally go with a vague "Worse than hives."

Tommy nods again. He seems pretty impressed. Well, he hasn't seen anything yet.

"Did you know I have a song about you and your allergies?"

His mouth falls open as I start improvising a fast and silly ditty, making up the words as I go along.

"*Iiiiiiiiiiif Tommy eats strawberries, his nose gets runny,*

Tommy is my allergy buddy! If I go in the sun, it'll mean my end; thank God I have Tommy as my allergy friend!"

Tommy giggles.

"If you think that was good, just wait until you hear the chorus," I tell him, and I launch into it.

"Doo-da-doo-da-doo-ACHOO!    Doo-da-doo-da-doo-ACHOO! Tommy's my allergy buddy."

He's grinning from ear to ear as his mom ushers him away. He turns and waves good-bye, the big smile still there. There's no way anyone will be more into me tonight than that little dude. So now is probably a good time to try out one of my newer songs. That way I can see where it needs tweaking without anyone noticing if (when) I mess it up.

I open my trusty notebook—full of the lyrics and chords to songs I've written, and basically my other best friend, next to Morgan—and flip to the page where I've scribbled my latest. I take a deep breath and go for it. After a false start, I go again and everything's working. My voice weaves through the music and I get totally lost in the moment. For the time being, it doesn't matter that I'm singing only to myself, that I have this rotten disease, and that I'm not at a wild and crazy graduation party like I should be right now.

When I look up from the frets of my guitar, it's like the apocalypse has happened, because life will never be the same. Charlie Freaking Reed is standing right in front of me. Watching me like he's actually interested. Listening to a song that's pretty much about him, if I'm being honest.

I go into total spaz mode and screech, "Oh my God!"

"Hi," he says, laughing at my overreaction.

That's it: hi. Yeah, maybe not the most original line. But it doesn't make a bit of difference; I'm still completely flustered and in awe that it's really him here in person after I've watched him from afar for so long. My pulse starts racing so fast that I'm convinced I'm going to pass out. I jump up and try to shove my guitar back in the case. The bag of Skittles plops to the ground.

The plan is to run away as fast as I can. I have absolutely zero experience talking to the hottest guy on the planet. Make that any guy older than Tommy, my number one superfan, no matter his level of attractiveness. I'll talk to Charlie Reed some other time, when my brain isn't a scrambled, panicked mess.

"Hey, I didn't mean to freak you out," Charlie says, handing the candy back to me. Our fingers touch. A wave of tingling energy runs up my arm.

The fight-or-flight adrenaline coursing through my

veins retreats enough for my brain to register that I need to chill out. "What?! Um. That's—no. Me freak? Never. I'm not a freak. I mean I never freak."

I'm not sure what language I'm trying to speak but it's definitely not English. This is not the way I envisioned us meeting. What a complete, epic failure. My instinct is to walk away because that makes sense. Finally get the chance to hang out with the amazing boy you've been drooling over for the past ten years? Refuse to speak to him. Smooth move!

To my horror, Charlie is still talking to me. "Hey, where are you going?"

"Home," I tell him. "I gotta get home."

It's not a lie. My dad is probably all over Find My iPhone, tracking the little dot that is me. In fact, he has probably been tracking me the entire time I've been at the train station. I wouldn't put it past him to ask Fred to broadcast my whole set on Facebook Live so he can watch me sing and monitor me all at the same time.

Charlie cocks his head and gives me a curious stare. I'd say he looks like the most adorable puppy ever, but he's cuter than even the cutest pug, something I didn't even know was possible. "Where do you live?" he asks. "You don't go to Purdue High."

I still can't get the latch on my case closed. My bad first impression is turning into a worse second and third impression. I try to hurry away.

"Nope. Nope, nope, nope. Different high school," I babble. Told you it was a bad habit. "But it's graduation night and my dad's a big worrier, so…"

The guitar case is finally locked up tightly. My escape is imminent. Maybe someday Charlie will forget how lame I acted tonight and we can start from scratch without all the mortifying word vomit on my part.

But then the case unlatches again as I stand up. My beloved grad present starts tumbling to the ground. My mom's guitar is about to be smashed to bits.

Charlie catches it at the last second. He places it gently back inside the case and closes it tightly. Then he picks up the Skittles for a second time and hands both the case and the candy back to me.

His eyes stare into mine until I'm pretty sure I'm no longer a solid mass. I turn into some sort of a puddle person who will need to be mopped up later. If my life was a movie, we'd definitely start kissing now and, like, fireworks would shoot off in the background.

But it isn't, so Charlie just says, "I, uh, graduated today, too."

I will myself not to reply, *I know! I watched on my computer from my weirdly darkened room!*

Too bad what I actually say is even worse.

"Well, con-GRAD-uation!" Then I wince and mutter again, "Oh my God."

Charlie cracks up. "That's, like, the dorkiest joke I ever heard."

I really have to give up now and get out of here. "Yep, that's me. A dork. I gotta go."

"What's your rush?" he asks, staying in step with me.

I say the first thing that pops into my head. "Um, it's my cat."

Just to be clear: I do not now have a cat, nor have I ever had a cat. If my dad would allow it, I'd have a dog. A pug named Tug McPuggerson. But Dad says it's not fair to keep a puppy cooped up in the house all day long, and he's worried about the UV rays that would hit me every time I had to let the adorable guy out. So no go there.

"Your cat." Charlie grins at me, like he can see right into my lying brain.

"Yep," I continue, undeterred by the stupidity of what I'm saying. "It . . . died."

His brow furrows adorably as a puzzled look crosses his face. "So you're not actually in a *rush*, then . . ."

"No, I am, I have to...plan the funeral...for the cat that died," I stammer.

I am hopeless.

So I make another break for it. I refuse to say anything more ridiculous than what has already come out of my mouth. And this time I finally succeed in ditching the boy of my dreams.

I hear him calling after me. "Wait...what's your name?"

I don't answer. If he finds out, I'll never be able to deny I was the crazy girl talking about her fake dead cat the first time I met him. So I just keep going.

It's only after I am safely at home, done exaggerating to my dad about how I completely killed it at the train station, and am tucked neatly into my bed that the regrets start to come fast and furious. How could I have blown my chance with Charlie Reed so completely?

Welcome to the most embarrassing night of my life.

# 5

Morgan stops by to get the full scoop the next morning on her run before I go to sleep. I've already texted her the overview of my exchange with Charlie—which is embarrassing enough—but now she wants the down-and-dirty details straight from the dead-cat owner's mouth.

"A cat?" she screeches, making a horrified face at me.

I groan and shove a pillow over my head. Maybe if I bury myself under here for long enough, I'll wake up later and find out it was all just a horrible dream.

"A cat *funeral*!" Morgan sputters, laughing so hard now she almost falls off the desk chair she's spinning around in.

"Stop saying it out loud!" I yell from under the pillow. There's no way this is going to turn out to be just a nightmare if she keeps repeating all the dumb things I said last night.

Morgan gets up, walks across the room, and plops down on the bed next to me. I can't see any of this, but I know she's there from the ripples of laughter shaking the mattress. She puts a hand on my shoulder. "It's okay, Katie. I've actually heard that dead pets are an aphrodisiac."

I sit up and take the pillow off my face. "What was I *supposed* to say?"

"Anything else," she tells me. "Literally any other combination of words in the English language."

I know the cat story was ridiculous and lame, but I can actually think of a few sentences that would have been worse. "Really? Like 'Hey, I'm Katie, I've watched you from my window every day for the last ten years'?"

"I mean, I wouldn't *start* with that…"

I cross my arms and give her a hard stare. "Okay, how about this, then. 'You may recall me from Purdue Elementary, where everyone referred to me as Vampire Girl.'"

Morgan rolls her eyes at me. "No one remembers that!"

I sigh and punch my pillow. "I've always wanted to talk to him and I've always wanted to see him in real life and then I finally got to and I froze. My body betrayed me. You betrayed me!" I yell, staring down at myself in disgust.

"You'll make up for it next time," Morgan says, her voice softening. She's not laughing at me anymore. She knows how much last night could have meant to me, and how crappy I feel for screwing it all up.

I give her a look. "You saw my tweet." I'm referring to the one I made last night after I got home: **Ugh. Never going out again. I mean it.**

"Katie, this is actually a good thing, you'll see," Morgan says. "Now you know you can go out and interact with people our age and not everyone is a mean-ass bully. You're very likable. Even when you say dumb stuff about your dead cat to the hottest guy in school."

"Stop reminding me!" I say, smacking myself in the forehead with my palm. I really think I might cry now. "Besides, all last night proved is that I'm completely socially inept after being stuck in the house all these years. I refuse to embarrass myself like that ever again."

Morgan pats my knee. "So you're a little rusty. All

the more reason to get back out there. Who knows what exciting thing might happen next time?"

"There's not gonna be a next time," I grumble. "At least not with Charlie."

"You don't know that—"

I stop her before she can give me any untrue reasons for why things might possibly work out in the future. "Yeah, I do. That was my shot. I'm never gonna see him again. And I know that for a fact because I'm never leaving the house again. My dad will be so relieved!"

"Come on now," Morgan says. "You don't really mean that."

I cross my arms over my chest. "Yes, I do."

She stops trying to convince me I'm anything but a total fail at boys and life on the outside in general, and starts scrolling through her phone instead. Her jaw drops and she looks back up at me with saucer eyes. "Have you checked out Dear Gabby today?"

My heart shifts into high gear. This can mean only one thing. I wrote a question to our favorite advice columnist months ago, thought about sending it every day, but refused until a moment of weakness—not to mention acute loneliness—got me late one night a few weeks ago. I never thought I'd actually get a response, so I have no idea how to deal with the news that my frighteningly honest and embarrassingly revealing thoughts are out there in a public forum for anyone to read. I head straight into denial.

"No," I mumble, fighting the urge to rip the phone out of Morgan's hands to assess the damage. "I don't really follow Dear Gabby anymore."

Morgan screws up her mouth and gives me her best sassy face. "So you're telling me you *didn't* write this letter? And that some other random girl with a condition that sounds like XP who sounds exactly like you did?"

I refuse to meet her eyes and pretend to be totally engrossed in picking fuzzies off my baby blanket instead.

"Fine. This totally isn't you," she says, and starts reading the words I already know. My heart is hammering against my rib cage now like it's trying to jump out and run away from this mortifying situation. "*Dear Gabby, First, the bad news: I have a life-threatening illness where my body can't deal with UV rays. Now the good news: Other than flipping day and night—if I can't go out in the sun, I might as well enjoy the stars—I live a normal life for the most part. I play guitar, hang out with my BFF, kill it in school (I'm graduating with a 4.0 and am now taking college classes), and have a great relationship with my dad.*

"The only thing missing is that special someone—I'm no different from anyone else when it comes to wanting to find a deep and magical connection. But barring dating a vampire who's centuries too old for me, what guy would ever be able to deal with the strange hours I keep? Not to mention the fact that we'd never be able to go on a beach vacation together?

"Despite everything I have working against me, there is someone I'd like to get to know better. He has no idea I exist, but I've watched him from a distance for years and have always been drawn to what appears to be his kindness and good humor. He's also ridiculously cute.

"So, Gabby, give it to me straight: Should I just give up on the idea of love, specifically with this boy? Or make a grand gesture to get his attention and hope he's cool with my genetic malfunction? Signed, Sunless but not Hopeless."

Morgan looks back up from her phone. I'm blushing from head to toe. I shake my head furiously. "Nope. No, no, no. Not me."

"So I guess that also means you have no interest in Dear Gabby's reply then, huh?" Morgan says, a little smile playing around her lips.

I'm still trying to play it cool. I don't even know why.

Clearly this letter was written by me. "I mean, if you think it's a good one, I'll read it," I mumble. "If you really want me to. I guess."

She smirks. "You're not going to like how Dear Gabby totally, one hundred percent agrees with my advice to you. Oh, I mean, that other girl with XP who's living a parallel life to yours. You have to... I mean *she* has to get back out there and try again with Charlie."

"Dear Gabby didn't say that!" I grab for Morgan's phone. She lets me have it. I start to read.

*Dear Sunless,*

*There's a not-so-famous adage a New Jersey–born friend once passed on to me: Everyone has their shit sandwich. The only difference is some people aren't willing to talk about it. Believe me when I tell you everyone comes into a relationship with baggage, and I mean everyone. Depression, dysfunction, debt, doubt, you name it. You just happen to have cells that can't process the sun and force you to be nocturnal. So what? Is that so much worse than anyone else's shit sandwich?*

*You might not be able to meet him for an afternoon of minigolf, but dating mostly goes on at night, anyway. Which means you're not out of the running as a potential partner—not by a long shot, pumpkin.*

*Besides, it seems to me you're putting the cart before the horse here. You're already assuming this guy—who you've said appears to be full of great qualities—would surely reject you because of a circumstance beyond your control. Remember, while you may not be out and about during daylight hours, he most certainly goes out at night. So why not put yourself somewhere he's apt to be and give him a chance to prove you wrong? Start a conversation. See where it leads. Be casual, cool, calm, collected. Allow yourself to be surprised.*

*I'm going to leave you with this thought. Actually, it's a challenge. Do not let this one aspect of your life—which doesn't define you, might I add—stop you from chasing your wildest dreams. Try putting a little more faith in yourself and your fellow humans, and our*

*infinite capacity to love and forgive each other*
*in spite of our shortcomings.*

    *As for this boy, I say go for it. In fact, go*
*for everything you want in this life. I hope*
*you get everything you dream of and more.*

*Love,*

*Gabby*

I ignore the part about not letting this one aspect of my life define me (because when you have a rare disease like XP, there's no getting away from it—but Gabby couldn't know about that) and try to let the solid advice sink in, but all I can think about is how vulnerable and exposed I feel. I pray Zoe Carmichael and her crew don't follow Dear Gabby. I'd hate to think how much more they'd be able to torture me with this kind of knowledge.

"The needing to have more faith in yourself and other people part, and our infinite capacity to love and forgive each other's shortcomings, is great, right?" Morgan says when I hand her back the phone. "I almost teared up, and you know how much it takes for me to get emotional."

"Personally, I liked the poop sandwich analogy," I say with a little smile. Dear Gabby really is the best. She's smart and honest, and always tells it straight even when you might not exactly want to hear it. "And I still contend I didn't write that."

Morgan eye-rolls me into the next century. "Sure," she says. "You know, it wouldn't kill you to talk to him again. You could, like, snap him a funny picture of one of your stuffed animals in a box and say you can hang out now that the funeral is over or something."

I shake my head. "Not even a chance."

"But he was so nice to you," Morgan protests. "He liked your song. And your voice. And you."

I think about that and come to the conclusion that Morgan's not completely off base. Charlie *was* really nice to me, despite all my awkwardness. He listened to my song and seemed to really appreciate it. He still wanted to talk to me even after I started making up insane lies to get away from him. He's pretty much the perfect guy... which is why he doesn't need me and my problems in his life, I quickly conclude. "Charlie Reed and I are just not in the cards," I tell her.

Morgan gets off my bed and grabs my guitar, then hands it to me. "You know what would be a great way to spend your time instead of being so stubborn? Write a song about last night. This is what Taylor Swift does!

She has awkward interactions with boys and then writes amazing songs about them."

So maybe there is a silver lining to this mortifying situation after all. Everyone knows heartbreak is a great source of artistic inspiration.

"Oh, you mean like this?" I take my guitar from Morgan and start improvising.

> *"I'm a crazy pathetic person, don't*
> *    know why,*
> *couldn't even look him in the eye,*
> *I choked, I blew it, felt like I'm gonna hurl,*
> *I'm the biggest dork in the whole wide*
> *    world…"*

"Hmmmm. I'd keep working on that," Morgan tells me.

I walk over to my guitar case, a new idea for a song forming in my head. I'm totally going to write a country tune called "My Fake Dead Cat (Wants You to Come to His Funeral)," which I will dedicate to Charlie Reed and he will hear it on the radio and laugh and find my awkwardness adorable and we'll start over. There's only one problem, though: My lyrics book isn't where it's supposed to be.

"Oh my God, my notebook!" I gasp, my heart racing into full panic mode. "I think I left it at the station. Every song I've ever written is in there! Can you go get it?"

"I would, but my parakeet died, and I have to sit shiva for him..."

I smack her on the thigh. "Seriously. Please."

She laughs. "Of course. I'll pick it up this afternoon."

• • •

Once Morgan takes off, I go back to wallowing in regrets of what might have been. Damn you, Charlie Reed. If only you'd been a total disappointment, I wouldn't care what an ass I made out of myself in front of you last night.

Unfortunately, you were even more awesome than I'd imagined.

**6**

Two disconcerting things happen later that day. First, I catch my dad sneaking back into the house after going to see my XP doctor without me. Again. This is not the first time it's happened.

"Dad!" I yell, rubbing my eyes and sitting up in bed when I hear his sneaky, creaky footsteps on the landing outside my bedroom. The clock reads six PM. The appointment with my XP doctor was at four. We were supposed to go together. WTF?

"Did you turn my alarm off?"

He hangs his head. "You just looked so peaceful sleeping there, and I thought you were probably overtired from playing at the station last night, so I made the executive decision to let you sleep in..."

"More like you can't deal with me going out in the day, ever, even though we know how to take the appropriate precautions," I say, raising an eyebrow and giving him an accusatory look. "Not to mention you hate when Dr. Fleming tells it to me straight."

He gives me a helpless little shrug. "She's such a pessimist! You don't need to hear negative messages, not when everything is going so well in your life."

*What life?* I think. But that's the kind of thing I would never say to my dad.

I pat the edge of my bed. He stares at it a bit, then reluctantly sits down. He looks like a little kid who got caught with his hand in the cookie jar.

"So what did she say?" I demand.

"Nothing, really. Wanted to know if there were any changes in your motor function or if you'd been exposed to the sun. Of course I said no."

I roll my wrist at him, like, *I know there's more, now*

*out with it.* "What about the study at the University of Washington?"

A big smile plants itself on my dad's face. "It's coming along! Anytime now!"

I know what this means, if only because it's happened so many times before. People aren't exactly flocking to fund research for a disease that affects only one in a million people. This drug trial most likely already ran out of money and therefore won't even reach phase two, which is when I'd have an opportunity to apply to be part of it. Or if by some miracle the study actually receives more funding, it would be even more of a miracle if I got chosen to participate in it. The futility of living with a disease no one cares—or even knows—about makes me want to scream. But that would be even more futile. It's an endless cycle of futility I'm dealing with here.

"Don't worry, I'm not holding my breath," I tell my dad. And then, because I want to knock that fake smile off his face, I say, "I'm sure Dr. Fleming also reminded you that any sun exposure at all will be the death of me and that kids with my kind of XP rarely live past twenty, am I right?"

Dad's face falls. "Of course not," he protests. "And if she did, I certainly wouldn't listen. Maybe you have a disease that affects one in a million, Katie, but you really *are* one in a million. None of those statistics apply to you. We're going to beat this thing. Together."

"Right," I say. But nothing ever changes when it comes to XP. There's not even a ray of hope. No new treatments. Just "stay out of the sun until the disease somehow finally gets you." I'm a prisoner of my genetic code, which sucks totally and completely.

"Katie, promise me you won't ever give up hope," he says, his voice cracking with emotion.

I look up and see Dad struggling to keep his composure. I wish we could actually talk about how little time I statistically have left and everything I want to accomplish during it. Come up with a game plan for quality of life, knowing that quantity is something we don't have much control over. But he just doesn't seem capable of it. I wonder, not for the first time, how my mom would've handled all of this. Since she died a few months before I was diagnosed, I'll never know, which means I'll always wonder. Would she have been better at facing the facts?

I don't like to think about it either. My expiration date, that is. Or what dying might be like. But I do sometimes. Of course I do. Usually late at night, when it's darker than dark and I'm the only one awake—in my house, on my block, in the city—I wonder if death is somehow similar and just as lonely. Like, just you, in the dark, awake and aware. I sincerely hope not, because that would be unnecessarily cruel. Like living my same life all over again, only for all of eternity.

So I force a smile on my face instead, and say, "You know I'd never do that, Dad. We're fighters. I'm not going anywhere."

He tries to smile back at me, but the color is still drained from his face, so I add, "Come on. You couldn't get rid of me if you tried."

"Good, because I don't think I could survive that," he says as he stands to leave. And there's that honesty I said I wanted. It breaks my heart along with my dad's.

• • •

I'm catching up on the latest posts in one of the rare-disease forums when Morgan sends me a text. **Got the notebook, but I had to run to work. I left it at the ticket counter.** I sigh. It's so Morgan not to have enough time to do both. I have an unproven theory that she has massive ADHD, what with all the twirling around she does in the desk chair in my room—that girl never sits still—and her absolute inability to be on time for anything. She claims I'm totally off base and that she's just a super-energetic person who tries to cram too many activities into too few hours. We've agreed to disagree on this one.

Still, I'm relieved I haven't lost basically an entire lifetime's worth of songwriting, and for all my grumbling inside my head, it's actually not a bad thing that I have to go get the notebook myself. I need to go for a walk and clear my head. Fresh air can cure almost anything, even being the cause of your dad's deep sorrow and royally screwing up meeting the guy of your dreams.

I pull on an oversize Seattle SuperSonics sweatshirt (the now-defunct basketball team my dad was obsessed with back in the day), a pair of ratty old jeans, and my black Converse. Downstairs, I find my dad simultaneously working on his laptop—probably inputting grades on the latest project he assigned his students—yelling at the Mariners game on TV, and eating a sandwich so stacked with meat that it's at least three inches high.

"I'm going to run to the station to pick up my notebook. I left it there last night. Fred has it."

Dad barely glances up at me, he's so engrossed in his sandwich. "Text me when you get there, be careful, and come right home. Love you," he says through a mouthful of ham and cheese. Sure, a quick back-and-forth trip is something he can handle, but any outing that holds the possibility that I might actually have some normal fun makes him a total basket case.

"Love you more," I tell him. And even though I get frustrated with him, I mean it.

He swallows in a big gulp, and before going in for another bite, he replies, "Not possible."

• • •

As I step out onto the porch and close the door behind me, I briefly let myself wonder where Charlie is right now, what he's doing, and with whom, before I silently start berating myself all over again for the dead-cat-funeral debacle. It doesn't matter what Charlie's up to, because we certainly won't be hanging out anytime soon.

I walk up the stairs to the train platform and head for the ticket counter. Fred's not in his usual spot. So I peek around the corner, thinking he might have left my notebook on the bench that's in front of where I normally set up.

I am right about that last part at least: My notebook *is* on the bench. Sitting in Charlie Reed's hands. He's flipping through it like it's a trashy gossip magazine that's already old news.

I don't know what's worse: Me babbling like an idiot when I finally meet the guy, or him manhandling what amounts to my most private thoughts. I am more humiliated than ever. I just have to figure out how to get the notebook back without him knowing I'm here, and I'll be on my way.

I dart behind a wall and call Morgan at work.

"Help!" I whisper the minute she picks up.

"Helloooooooo, Purdue Creamery," she trills. "How is your second date with Charlie going?"

"Wait, what?" I say, my mouth falling open. "How did you know he was here?"

"I gave him your notebook for safekeeping," she says, like that's a perfectly okay thing to do.

"I'm going to kill you, Morgan! How could you do this to me? I'm in a size XL SuperSonics sweatshirt! I didn't even brush my hair!"

Morgan just laughs. "Katie, I don't know how to tell you this but...you're super freaking hot. I can't even see you right now and I know you look gorgeous."

"That's not the actual case," I hiss. "And if you could see me, you'd agree."

"Katie, hold on a sec," she says, and then I hear her practically yell, "Excuse me! Can't you see I'm on the phone?"

I truly hope she's not talking to someone trying to order a cone; Morgan needs the extra cash from working at the ice cream shop for college. Getting herself fired would really be a problem. There aren't many other places to work in town, and it's small enough here that everyone would know she didn't leave her last job of her own accord.

"Please tell me that wasn't a customer," I say when she's back on the line.

"Oh, it was," she says. "A customer, and then that annoying geek I work with, Garver. He asks me like eight jillion questions a night. *What do you like to do for fun, Morgan? What's your favorite flavor of ice cream, Morgan? How many siblings do you have, Morgan? What's your favorite TV show, Morgan?* I swear, he's like a toddler with all his yapping."

"That's called being interested in your life." Leave it to her to hate any guy who shows an honest interest in her. Morgan tends to like bad boys who only ever talk about themselves. "That's called conversation."

"It's called one hundred percent annoying," she corrects me. "And now, as for Charlie, just be yourself, Katie. He's a nice guy. And he likes you, I can tell. Just promise me you'll try not to ramble, okay?"

By now I've come to terms with the fact that talking to him is pretty much my only option if I ever want to see my notebook again. I sigh. "Only if you try to be nice to this Garver guy. I feel sorry for him."

"Gross, no," she snorts. "Call me after."

She hangs up before I can say anything else.

Left with no other choice, I take a deep breath and start walking over to Charlie. I'm almost in front of him when he looks up and sees me. I'm rewarded with the biggest, most welcoming smile I've ever seen. He's got these perfect lips—not too pillowy, not too thin—that look like they've never been chapped a day in their life. His teeth are perfectly straight and white. His eyes are so warm and friendly that they make me feel like I'm drowning in an ocean of kindness. I'm so dazzled, I even forget for a second that I'm mad he invaded my personal space.

"You *are* real," he says. "I thought I might've dreamed you or something."

"Were you in the REM stage of sleep?" I say. He looks unsure of how to respond to my lame joke, so I plow ahead. "Just kidding. I mean, I know you weren't because I talked to you and you were awake. But that's when dreams happen, because your brain activity is high, and your eyes are actually moving the whole time behind your eye-lids, which is so weird, it looks like a typewriter or something..."

I stop short, realizing I've done it yet again. Charlie is grinning at me. Not in a mean way. Just, like, nice. Amused.

"Anyway, thanks for babysitting my notebook," I tell him, trying to grab it.

But he's gripping it too tightly. It stays in his possession. "I still don't know your name."

"It's Katie." I guess that's the secret password, because he hands my notebook over. I scan the pages to make sure nothing's changed. It looks okay, but I just have to ask. "Hey, you didn't actually read it, did you?"

"Maybe a little..."

Now I'm mortified and mad all over again. Maybe the girls at Purdue High let him get away with anything just because he's cute, but that's not how I roll. "Are you kidding me?"

"What?" His eyes are wide, like he's actually surprised I might not want him knowing what's in my journal.

"You can't just read people's stuff," I tell him, holding up the book as evidence. "This is like my diary, you know. Is that your move? You do that grin thing, and just because you're handsome, you think you can get away with invading people's privacy?"

Charlie grins that charming grin again. "You think I'm handsome?"

Shame burns up my cheeks and my ears. I'm blushing so hard I'm practically sweating. I'm hoping the fact that it's nighttime makes this less obvious.

Charlie holds up his hands. "Hey, the invasion of privacy was minimal and necessary. You left so fast, and I just wanted to see who it belonged to."

I stay silent. I'm not letting him off that easy.

"I like that you handwrite things," he adds softly. "It's old-school. It's cool."

And just like that, I'm, like, totally in love with him again. I can't help it. My major crush is no match for my minor anger. A little smile curves up my lips. "Well, thanks. For not invading it too much, I guess."

I consider that maybe Morgan and Dear Gabby were right. Maybe I do need to give Charlie—and other people my own age—a chance to surprise me. After all, tonight went relatively smoothly. I turn to leave, proud of myself for handling the situation so well without all the talk about dead cat funerals this time.

"Did another cat die?" he calls after me as I go.

I laugh and turn back around. "No, I'm just heading home."

"Can I walk with you?"

"Yeah, I guess so." I'm giddy with happiness on the inside but don't want to act anywhere near as enthusiastic as I'm feeling. Something tells me Charlie Reed has never had to work very hard to get a girl, and I need him to know I'm different. Not because of the XP, I mean, but just because I'm me. "Fine, okay."

We walk slowly down the middle of the road. There aren't any cars around to worry about, so we're just meandering and making small talk. Everything's quiet, and our footsteps echo off the sleepy houses we pass. It's nice. Comfortable.

"So you were homeschooled?" Charlie repeats after I tell him. "That's wild."

I think about all those nights my dad drilled me on the periodic table, or the constellations, or Latin conjugations. Charlie's assessment of homeschooling is so off base it's laughable. "It was kind of the exact opposite of wild," I tell him. Then I add, "My dad's really protective," even though I figure by now that this has got to be pretty clear.

Charlie looks left, right, up to the sky, then back at me. "He's not, like, watching us right now, is he?"

"Oh, totally. He's got a drone on us for sure."

He laughs. And then I laugh, mostly because I'm amazed I made *him* laugh. Who knew my life could go from the deepest depths of the dumps to this kind of amazing high all in a span of twenty-four hours?

"So I kind of need to know...what did you think?" I ask.

"Of your dad following us with a drone? It's kind of over-the-top, don't you think?"

I crack up again. "I meant, what did you think of the songs. That you read. Without my permission."

He shrugs. "I don't know, really. You can't *read* a song. I'd have to hear them."

I stop walking. We're nearly to my house, and ten bucks says my dad is standing in the living room alternately staring at his Find My iPhone app and out the front window, waiting for me to walk back through the door. The last thing I want to have to do is explain who Charlie is and why I'm out here with him.

"Is this your house?" he asks, pointing at the one right in front of us.

I gesture beyond where he thinks it is, a block farther

up the hill. "No, it's that one. But my dad is a pretty light sleeper, and I'd rather not wake him up."

Charlie stares at where I live. "I can't believe we've never met before. I've probably skated by your house like every day on the way to practice."

"Practice?" I ask, even though, of course, I know what he's referring to. How could I not know? He always had that Purdue Penguins backpack, his kickboard, and all sorts of miscellaneous swim gear tucked under one arm as he rode by. Not to mention the fact that his name was in the local paper every week when he would break records at the latest meets during the season.

"Yeah, I used to be a competitive swimmer." And just like that, the adorable spark in his eyes is extinguished.

"Used to be?"

Another shrug. "Story for another day."

I switch gears, hoping he goes back to being Mr. Happy-Go-Lucky again. "It's weird, right? That you know my house."

"Sure." Charlie still looks sad. The spell between us is broken. Maybe next time—if there is a next time—we'll get it back. As for now, I figure I should just disappear again.

"Well, I gotta go. Thanks for walking me home," I tell him.

I get only two steps up the hill when Charlie says maybe the ten greatest words in the English language.

"Hey, Katie. Would you maybe want to do something sometime?"

I whirl back around. "Together, you mean?"

Charlie laughs, back to his regular relaxed self. "No, I meant in general, by yourself, in life. Of course I meant us, together."

I worry about how I'll explain my extenuating circumstances to Charlie, and if my dad would even agree to let me go out with him, and whether I could keep my rambling to a minimum even if he did. But then I realize, this is Charlie Reed. Dream Boy. I have to try. For Morgan and Dear Gabby, but especially for me.

"I...I'm pretty busy during the day. I'm really free only at night," I tell him, skipping over all the complicated parts.

"I can be free at night," he says with an adorable little shrug.

"Put your number here, then," I say, walking back over to him and flipping through my notebook to find a spot for him that's not full of doodles and lyrics and chords. And then I see it. He's already printed his name neatly on the first available blank page. His digits are right next to it.

I stop short. "Ooooooooh. Oh, that was smooth."

Charlie gives me another heart-melting grin. "Another one of my moves. I'm old-school."

And then we just stand there smiling at each other. After a while, it gets kind of awkward that neither one of us is making a move to leave. So I say good-bye for real this time and run up the hill to my house.

I have a date! With Charlie Reed! I turn back around to wave good night to him and discover he's still standing there, watching me and smiling. Instead of feeling embarrassed this time, I feel all warm and toasty. Like a fire has been lit inside me.

Me. Charlie Reed asked *me* out.

This is all new—liking an actual real-live Charlie and not just the figment of him outside my window, and him quite possibly liking me back. It's kind of scary. In a good way.

I think I like it.

# 7

Morgan bursts into my room the next after-noon right when I'm getting up. "TELL. ME. EVERY-THING."

I've, of course, already texted her what happened, but she wants to hear it from my mouth. She sprawls across my bed as I try to get all the words and Charlie's expressions just right. I describe the way the moon danced between us as we walked home, how he asked me on a date, and how his name and number were already in my notebook, so it must have been premeditated, not just like a whim or, worse, a mistake. She's grinning at me and I'm grinning at her and I feel stupid but stupidly happy, too.

"That's so romantic it disgusts me," she says when I finish.

I sigh and throw a hand over my heart. It's beating faster than normal even a day later. "I know. It was perfect."

Morgan sits up and grabs my hands. "So he was cool about your XP, huh? I had a feeling about him. I knew he wouldn't be a jerk about it. That's the only reason I let him give you back your notebook, I swear. I never would've let him put his grubby paws on it otherwise."

I start biting a fingernail. I'm trying to be casual and avoid telling her the truth, but Morgan knows me way too well.

"No. Katie, come on now," she groans. "You didn't tell him? You, like, think he's not gonna find out when you start melting in front of him like the Wicked Witch of the West? Boys are dumb but not *that* dumb."

I wince. "It didn't come up."

"What do you mean, it didn't come up?" Morgan yells.

I clap a hand over her mouth. Dad definitely does not need to know I (a) like a boy who (b) asked me to hang out with him after (c) I neglected to tell him about my craptastic medical condition. She sticks her tongue out and starts licking my hand until I drop it from her face.

"I mean," I say in a whisper, hoping she'll get the hint to tone it down in here, "he didn't ask me if I had a genetic disorder where sunlight will kill me and I did not say yes."

Morgan starts to say something else, but I jump back in before she can start giving me a hard time again.

"Listen to me. When people find out you're sick, you stop being a person and become, like, a cause. And it ruins everything."

For once in her life, Morgan can't think of a snappy comeback. She just nudges me with her foot. I understand she means, *Dude, I know. It sucks*. I give her a little smile because I know she knows, at least as best she can. She sees how much I struggle with not being able to do the things I want to do. But we also both know there's not a damn thing either of us can do about it.

"I promise I'll tell him. The next time I see him, okay? Not that I know when that will be..."

"Oh, I do," Morgan tells me, jumping up off my bed. "You know the annoying guy who works with me at the ice cream shop?"

"The nerdy one you hate? Who is also clearly in love with you?"

"Eww, will you stop saying that?" she protests. "And, yes, Garver. His parents are out of town and he's throwing a party tonight and he told me to bring friends. So I'm gonna bring you, and you're gonna bring Charlie."

Tonight? I'm so not prepared for this. I need some time to find just the right outfit, maybe get a haircut, and, I don't know, buy some makeup and figure out how to apply it since I don't usually go anywhere that would require a fancy face and have zero clue where to start.

"What? No, no, no. I can't—that's not—don't I have to wait for him to call me or something?"

"Totally." Morgan nods. "And then his squire will send a note via pigeon asking if you'd like to merge your kingdoms. What is this, eighteenth-century England? You're a hot, young, badass woman in charge of her own life, and you text him whenever you damn well please!"

She tosses me my phone. "Just be confident. Give him the facts."

I stare at the phone. My mind is as blank as the screen. There's no way I'm doing this.

"If you don't text him, I will," Morgan warns.

I know she'll make good on the threat, so I start

typing. I go with the first thing I can think of, no editing or second-guessing myself. **Hey, my friend is having a party tonight if you want to come.** I hit send before I can chicken out.

"But play a little hard to get," Morgan says the minute my message shoots into the stratosphere.

Fine. I type some more. **I don't care if you come or not.** Send. There. All better.

"And make sure he knows he's not the only reason you're going," she continues.

**I have lots of friends,** I quickly add. Geez, why does this have to be so complicated?

Morgan grabs my phone and reads my masterpiece. She groans.

"What?"

"Remember the dead cat?"

I nod.

"This is the same," she tells me.

"No, it's not!" I screech.

"He's going to think that not only do you not like him, but you actually hate him," Morgan tells me.

"Fix it, then!"

Before she can start cleaning up my mess, my phone

buzzes. Morgan glances at it and then back up at me. She's grinning.

"Never mind. Well played, my friend. Well played."

"What?" I'm more confused than ever. "I seriously don't understand how any of this works."

She holds up my phone so I can read the screen. There's Charlie's reply. I'm in.

I can't stop smiling. I don't know how it worked or why, but it did. "Now we have to convince my dad to actually let me go," I whisper, aiming a thumb at my closed door.

"Leave it to me," Morgan says, and runs out of my room to talk to him.

I catch up with her just in time to hear him saying, "I don't think it's a good idea, Morgan. I don't know the parents, we don't know what kind of party it is, Katie doesn't even know these kids."

He's rushing around the kitchen, emptying the dishwasher, putting away dishes, straightening up the cutlery drawer, anything but making actual eye contact.

"I know Garver!" Morgan protests. "I work with him. He's a complete goober. This is gonna be a tame, safe, parent-friendly party."

My dad stops the busywork for a second, a smile lighting up his formerly worried face. "That sounds so boring! How about I order Chinese and put on Netflix—"

"Dad!" I bark. It comes out harsher than I intended it to. My father's face crumples. I can't stand how his entire existence seems to hinge on protecting me from the most benign things on the planet. I'm eighteen, not a toddler who might go barreling into a glass coffee table or tumble down the stairs if she's left to her own devices too long. The sun won't get me. I can go to a nerdy party without disaster striking. I *need* him to understand this.

"I'm a good kid. You know I'm not gonna do anything crazy," I continue, more gently this time. "But if I stay here for one more night listening to everyone else living their life outside my window, I might *go* crazy."

My voice cracks and I have to pinch myself so I don't start crying. I normally work very hard at not feeling sorry for myself and being grateful for what I have, but now that I've gotten the teensiest, tiniest taste of "normal," it's like there's no turning back. I need more than just the four walls of my bedroom and my guitar to be happy. I need an actual life.

"Please, please, let me feel normal." I'm not above begging to get what I want, which is to spend more time with Charlie Reed. "I'll text you every hour. And tomorrow we can order too much lo mein and have a movie marathon."

My dad sighs and opens his mouth. I'm sure there's some other lame but well-meaning excuse on the tip of his tongue about why I shouldn't go. I preempt it by throwing my arms around him and giving him a huge bear hug.

"Thank you! Thank you! You're the best dad in the world!"

"If you're saying that, then I'm definitely making the wrong decision," he mutters.

Still, he doesn't say no. So I grab Morgan's hand and we run up to my room before he can change his mind. My phone buzzes along the way.

"Okay, Charlie says he'll meet us at Garver's at eight," I tell Morgan.

She gasps. "We gotta get ready!"

I check my watch. "We have three hours."

"Oh my GOD, we're already behind!"

This is a weird turn of events, since Morgan is about the lowest-maintenance person in the world. Normally, she wears jeans and a casual T-shirt, then slaps a knit beanie on her head and voilà! She's out the door.

"Who are you and what have you done with my best friend?"

"Dude. You are meeting up with the guy you've lusted after for a decade—"

I raise my eyebrows. "I hardly think I was lusting after him when I was eight years old; that's not even a thought eight-year-olds have—"

"Semantics," she says with a wave of her hand. "You are hooking up with a guy you've loved for more than ten years—"

"Who said anything about hooking up? I literally have zero experience in that department. And it's not like I'm going to go from absolutely nothing to positively everything just because my dad is finally letting me go to a party!"

"I wasn't implying you have to do anything you don't want to do," Morgan says. "Though I do think it would be a total waste for a gorgeous girl like you to have to die a virgin—"

"OH MY GOD, MORGAN!" I whisper-scream. "I am not losing my virginity to a guy I've talked to exactly twice in my life. And thanks for the vote of confidence, but I'm not planning on dying anytime soon either."

An awkward moment passes. We have these a lot because even though we basically tell each other everything, we leave a lot unsaid.

"Look, all I'm saying is tonight is a big deal," she tells me. "This is, like, what you've always dreamed of. You just said it to your dad—you get to be *normal* for once. But I happen to think you've waited too long to settle for just normal. Tonight is going to be fan-fucking-tastic, and so are you."

"It is? I am?"

She nods. "Yup. No doubt."

Morgan walks over to my closet and starts rifling through it. She doesn't have a lot to work with. Honestly, most days I sit around in leggings and a sweatshirt, because why not be comfy if you're not going anywhere?

"Is this the sum total of your clothing?" she calls from inside, her voice echoing against the walls.

"Yeah, unless you count the two dresses I ordered when I thought my dad was going to let me go to that concert with you in Seattle, but then he said no because we'd have to leave before the sun went down," I tell her. "I keep forgetting to ask him to send them back. Probably wishful thinking that he was going to change his mind."

Morgan pops her head back out of the closet. "Where are they?" she demands. "And why did you need two? Planning a wardrobe change so the paparazzi wouldn't catch you wearing the same thing for more than an hour at your Seattle debut?"

I laugh. "I was going to pick the one that looked best and return the other one. But then I didn't have to pick either, and I forgot to return both."

I grab the box from under my bed and hand it to her. She first pulls out a super body-con black romper with a strappy back. I don't know how I ever thought my dad would let me out of the house wearing it, so good thing it became a moot point. Next, she holds up a sweet ivory lace dress. It's still short and sexy, but in a much more ladylike and classy way.

Morgan tosses me the sweet outfit. "If you're so desperate to hold on to your virginity, I'd go with this one."

Truth: It's a great choice for what I have planned, which is making Charlie Reed fall madly in love with me. I head into the bathroom. Stripping off my usual leggings-and-T-shirt combo, I shimmy into the dress and zip it up.

I check myself out in the mirror, hoping I've somehow turned into a ravishing supermodel. Nope. I look pretty much the same as always, only with a beautiful outfit on. Awkward.

I step out to show Morgan, wincing. "I feel so stupid. Like I'm a little kid who raided my mommy's closet."

Morgan cocks her head and gives me a long stare. "It's absolutely perfect."

"How can you say that?" I protest. "It's just plain old me with fancy wrapping on."

"*Psshhhh*. Finding the right outfit is just the first part of getting ready," she says. "We still have to do your hair and makeup. By the time I'm finished, you won't even recognize yourself."

It's funny, because like I said, Morgan is the consummate tomboy tough girl in the way she dresses and acts, but who knew she had such a handle on contouring and winged eyeliner and BB cream and lip kits and whatever? (I do a lot of late-night online shopping. Can't imagine I'm the only one...) She applies it all to my face like she's a professional makeup artist.

One minute, I look like some weird zoo animal with different colored stripes on my cheeks and forehead; the next, everything's blended and I look insanely natural but also so much more polished than when I roll out of bed in the morning.

I stare some more at the expert makeup job. It's truly impressive. "I don't get how you did that."

• • •

Morgan bounds down the stairs first, with me following close on her heels this time. My father is standing in the foyer staring up at us. His mouth falls open. I hope that means *You look pretty*, not *March back up to your room and scrub that makeup off, young lady.*

"May I present Katherine Price of Washington," Morgan announces like we're making our society debut at some fancy ball.

My dad still says nothing.

"Does this look silly?" I ask. "'Cause I can go change."

My dad clears his throat. "You look amazing, Peanut," he finally says, a little catch in his voice. "You're a beauty. Just like your mom."

I smile. It's the exact right thing to say to me. The exact thing I needed to hear in this moment. He watches us as we run out of the house. I turn back around and give him a huge smile. *I'm gonna be fine.*

I truly know it. From the look on his face, I think even my dad believes it this time. I grab Morgan's hand and hustle us out of sight before he can change his mind.

# 8

Garver's house isn't far from mine. Even walking slowly, plotting out with Morgan how I should play things with Charlie tonight, we get there in ten minutes. The old Victorian has a wraparound front porch complete with a swing that looks perfect for soaking up sunny days while watching the world go by. I'd love to enjoy that kind of simple pleasure. It makes me kind of mad to think that people who can often don't.

Garver appears at the door without us even having

to knock. He's of average height and weight, and has longish dark curly hair, a cute little-boy face, and zero zits. There's no major geekiness to him that I can detect, other than maybe his WHY AM I HERE T-shirt. He's certainly not anywhere near as dorky as Morgan always claims.

Garver's eyes light up when he sees her. "You came!" he yelps.

"Don't sound so excited," she says. "Or I might change my mind."

I press my foot down on top of her toes. *Be nice.* She wriggles her shoe out from under mine without acknowledging my silent message.

"Any chance you or your hot friend knows how to get beer out of a keg?"

Morgan pushes past Garver, dragging me behind her. She stops short in the kitchen. Two of Garver's friends—one with a bowl cut and wearing a bow tie, the other with Mr. Spock eyebrows and mustard-colored flood pants—are trying to pry the thing open with a dinner knife.

Morgan stares at Garver incredulously. "You didn't get a tap?"

He shrugs, palms up. "I didn't know they were separate things! Why would they sell me a barrel of beer I couldn't access?"

Morgan spins around the kitchen, then peeks into the living room. Her face falls and she mouths *Sorry* at me. She's horrified, and she's not even trying to hide it.

"Garver, what the hell?! This really is a tame, safe, parent-friendly party!"

Garver points over to the kitchen table. On it are a few gallons of ice cream, a can of whipped cream, some sprinkles, and a squirt bottle of Magic Shell. "Do tame parties have *sundae bars*?"

Morgan smacks him. I watch his friends—who from the looks of them probably are going to be actual rocket scientists someday—have zero luck liberating the beer from the barrel. Like, they'll probably figure out how to populate Mars, but they cannot get beer out of a keg. The thought makes me laugh out loud.

"This is so cool!" I whoop.

"Don't listen to her," Morgan tells Garver as she grabs my arm and starts dragging me away. "She's never been to a party before, so she doesn't realize how dire this situation is. We're outta here."

Garver runs ahead of us and cuts Morgan off before

she can get out the front door. "You're leaving?! But I made a huge thing of chili."

Morgan rolls her eyes at him. "Chili is not a party food!"

There's a knock at the door. Relief is written all over Garver's face. "You see? Party's just kicking off." He checks out who it is through the peephole. "Wait. Whoa. What is Charlie Reed doing here?"

Before I can say I invited him, Garver throws the door open. He welcomes Charlie, pats him on the back like an old pal, and ushers him inside.

Charlie looks right past him and our eyes meet. *Whoosh.* We're totally locked into each other. Nothing else seems to matter. Everyone else ceases to exist.

"Wow," he whispers. "Hi."

Something about the look on his face makes me think Morgan deserves a huge tip for my makeover. She's nudging me with an elbow and grinning at us grinning at each other. I know what she means. It's hard to miss how much we're vibing.

"Hi," I say back.

Staring at Charlie is like staring right into the sun— and we all know how dangerous that would be for me— so I have to pry myself away. I glance into the kitchen where Mr. Spock Eyebrows has decided it's a great idea to bring a rolling pin down on the keg. Of course, it bounces off the barrel—that thing must be made of, like, titanium—and hits him right in the face. And still there is no beer. Bruises probably, but no beer.

I'm momentarily grateful this isn't some huge rager where I'd also have to contend with talking to people who actually know how to tap a keg and don't serve sundaes and chili as party food. Safe, tame, and parent friendly is about all I can handle at this particular moment.

Next, the guys get a mallet, some sort of spike, and a roll of duct tape. They line up the random items on the counter like surgical instruments. I sigh. It's going to be a while.

"Maybe we should go sit on the porch while these guys figure that thing out?" I suggest.

Charlie follows me outside and sits down next to me on the swinging bench, and we float gently back and forth. I'm staring up at the sky. He's staring at me.

"You look amazing," he says.

"It's all Morgan," I tell him with a wave of my hand, trying to shoo away the compliment and all the embarrassing blushing that accompanies it.

He shakes his head. "Nope."

I'm about to protest again when Garver bursts onto

the porch. He's holding two bowls of chili. I don't want to hurt his feelings, but I also don't want to have chili breath around Charlie.

"For you, good sir," Garver says, handing one to each of us. "And for you, mademoiselle."

"Oh, thank you so much, but I can't. I'm...allergic," I tell him.

"I'm allergic to your dead cat, but that doesn't stop me from hanging out with you, right? Try it, you'll like it," Charlie says with a wink.

He takes a bite, swallows, and gives Garver a thumbs-up. "Top shelf, buddy."

Garver tries again to hand off the bowl to me, but I put my hands up. "No. Thanks. Really."

"You sure?" he asks.

I nod, so he starts chowing it down instead. Charlie makes a face, leans over, and whispers, "Wise decision. It tastes like ass."

I'm still giggling at Charlie's assessment when Morgan walks outside. Garver stops midgobble to stare at her. A blob of beef teeters precariously on his chin.

"I really thought we'd have a bigger turnout," Garver comments. "But more beer and chili for us, right?"

One of Garver's friends sticks his head out the front door and says, "I told you not to go up against a cheerleader!"

"What cheerleader?" Morgan asks.

"The mean blonde one with the big Cadillac," Garver says through a mouthful of food.

"Zoe Carmichael?" Morgan yelps.

*Thank God we're here and not there*, I think.

"Yeah. Zoe." Garver nods. "She's also having a party. Must have dinged our turnout."

"Should we just go there?" Charlie suggests.

Adrenaline shoots through my body. There's no chance I'm going to Zoe's party. But there's also no chance I'm *not* going if that's where Charlie's headed. What a conundrum.

Garver's shoulders slump. Anyone can see how important it is for him to impress Morgan. Which he's not, but at least he's trying. If we all leave, it's not even a possibility anymore. "Whoa. You're gonna bail on me, brah?"

"Nobody's bailing. I just thought we could move this whole scene over to her house." Charlie looks over at me to gauge my reaction.

I avoid his stare and look at Morgan like *What am I*

*supposed to do now?* She looks at me and shakes her head. I look back at Charlie and shake mine.

"You know how I told you my dad is superstrict? Well, I can't go anywhere but where I said I'd be or I'll be grounded for the entire summer."

"Couldn't you just, like, text him and say your plans changed?" Charlie asks.

I shrug. "That's not how it works with my dad. Like I told you, he's pretty overprotective."

"Let me drive you home and we can explain it to him together," he offers.

More emphatic head shaking from me. My dad doesn't even know Charlie exists. The last thing I want to do is have to explain who he is, how we met, and that now we want to hit a rager together.

"Okay then, staying here it is," Charlie says, and he doesn't even seem mad about it.

• • •

After a half an hour, the keg is still untapped, the chili's been eaten, and we've all demolished sundaes from Garver's elaborate sundae bar. Charlie and I are left staring at each other, the conversation petering down to nothing. I am desperate not to let my first real date with him be my last one. And if this night gets any sleepier, I'm pretty sure that's a distinct possibility.

"Let's just go," I suddenly blurt out. "To the other party. What my dad doesn't know won't hurt him."

Morgan gives me a look like *Have you completely lost your mind?* I wince. Desperate times call for desperate measures.

"Okay, cool," she says, giving me the hairy eyeball. "Lemme just get my passport, because Zoe Carmichael is Satan and her home is most likely the portal to hell."

Garver lets out a laugh.

"Shut up, Garver, that wasn't even a good joke," she says, trying to act like she doesn't love that he totally appreciates her humor. "And, Katie, you do realize we're talking about Zoe *Carmichael* here? You know, the girl who basically ruined—"

I cut her off before she can say "your life" or utter the words "Vampire Girl." "I'm sure it'll be fine," I say quickly.

"Zoe's harmless," Charlie assures us both. "She's like a gnat with a really expensive car."

Morgan grabs my arm and pulls me up off the swing. "We'll be back in a second, guys," she says, and drags me into the house.

I follow, glancing over my shoulder at Charlie as we

walk away. He has a totally confused look on his face. I shrug like *I don't know either.*

"You do not have to go to Zoe's just because you think that's what Charlie wants to do," she says when we get inside.

"I know that." I stare down at my feet and shuffle them around a bit. "I kind of just want to see what an actual high school party is like. No offense to Garver. He's nice. The ice cream was good. But even I think it's kind of lame here. This party is only slightly more exciting than watching Netflix with my dad."

Morgan grabs my chin and pierces me with an intense stare. "You're sure?"

I nod, gripping her hands in mine and taking a deep breath. "I'm sure. Dear Gabby inspired me. I can't let XP hold me back anymore."

Morgan sighs and sticks her hands on her hips. "You are so full of shit."

"I'm not going if you don't go," I add.

"You suck, Katie," she says.

"I'm not trying to," I tell her. "I can't help it. I found out I like being normal. Sorry."

Morgan gives me an exasperated look and walks out onto the porch. I follow her back there.

"So?" Charlie asks when he sees us.

"Still undecided," Morgan says. "I mean, Garver put out such a nice spread..."

Garver hops to his feet. "Um, Charlie and I discussed it, and we think it's in all of our best interest to move this thing to another venue."

"You don't have to put on a front, Garver," Morgan tells him. "If you'd rather we stay here, we're all down. Seriously."

Garver shakes his head. "No, honestly. Let's roll."

Morgan still looks unconvinced.

Charlie starts chanting, "Mor-gan. Mor-gan. Mor-gan."

Garver and I pick it up a beat later, so now we're a chorus of encouragement. "MOR-GAN! MOR-GAN! MOR-GAN!"

"Fine," she finally concedes. "But don't come crying to me when Zoe condemns you all to an existence of eternal fire and brimstone."

We all cheer. I throw my arms around her.

"You're the best friend anyone could ever ask for," I whisper in her ear.

"I honestly hope you don't live to regret this," she whispers back. "But just know I'll be there even if you do. To throw down with anyone who dares to mess with you— and also to tell you I told you so."

It's such a classic Morgan thing to say. I pull back and grin at her. "Got it."

Garver whistles, and yells to his friends, "Let's go, boys! We're mobilizing!"

• • •

Before I have any more time to reconsider my impulsive decision, we pull up to a huge waterfront mansion. There's a shiny white Escalade parked in the driveway. Its license plate reads 2LIT4U. It's got to be Zoe's. Clearly, she hasn't changed a bit. I'm really starting to have second thoughts, but it's too late to turn back now.

Charlie easily lifts the keg out of Garver's friend's trunk and places it on the ground. The guys stare at him like he's Superman since it took all three of them to get it *in* the trunk, and they start rolling it awkwardly toward the impressive home, which is buzzing with loud music and even louder people. The closer we get to the front door, the slower they roll until everything's at a total standstill.

Garver clears his throat nervously. "This may not be a good idea," he says. "We've never even talked to Zoe."

"I have," Morgan says. "And you're not missing anything except a brush with evil."

"Relax, guys," Garver's friend with the bowl cut and bow tie says. "I talked to Zoe just last week."

"Do you mean when she almost hit you with her SUV and called you a douchebag?" Garver asks, his mouth hanging open like even he can't believe how clueless his friend is. "That's not an actual conversation."

"Yes it is!" Bowl Cut and Bow Tie protests. "I said 'Sorry' to her. It was a back-and-forth. We were talking."

"It'll be fine," Charlie assures them. "Let's do it."

His hand reaches for mine. I take it and we start heading up the stairs to the front door. We all stand on the porch as Charlie takes the heavy brass door knocker with a giant lion's head carved into it and gives the door a few loud raps. With my hand in Charlie's, I feel safe and cared for, like nothing bad can happen. Even if we were actually approaching the gates of hell, I think I'd go there with him.

# 9

When Zoe appears at the door, memories of all the times she gave me crap hit me hard, and I have to bite my lip to keep from gasping out loud. She looks just like I remember, only, of course, age progressed and even more beautiful.

Her eyes scan past me like I don't exist, lighting up when she sees Charlie. An odd pang of jealousy hits me, which is dumb, because it's not like I have any claim on him. This is our first date—for all I know, it could also be our last.

"I was wondering where you were!" she exclaims in a sweet voice that's probably not the one she uses on a regular basis. She's clinging to Charlie's arm like they're on the *Titanic* and it's sinking.

"Hey," he replies, carefully removing his arm from hers. "Yeah, sorry I'm late. We were pregaming at Garver's."

Zoe wrinkles her nose as she assesses who Charlie just admitted to hanging out with rather than her: me, some chick she most likely thinks she's never seen in her life; Morgan, who glares back at her, ready to rip her eyeballs out if she makes the slightest rude comment; and three boys she'd never give a second look. "Sorry, who are these people?"

"My friends," Charlie says with a shrug. Zoe hovers in the doorway, her face registering something close to disgust. She looks like she's ready to slam the door shut in our faces when Charlie adds, "We brought a keg."

Garver goes to lift it up as proof; it barely moves. Then he and his friends try together and finally get the thing as far as waist high.

Zoe scowls but finally steps aside to let us in. I exhale a long, slow breath. Crisis averted, at least for now. She seems to have zero idea I'm actually the Vampire Girl she tortured all those years ago.

Garver and his buddies somehow manage to get the keg into the kitchen, and I hear a loud cheer. The geek brigade are now beer heroes, welcome to stay as long as they can keep the party going.

I follow Charlie into the living room. Kids are packed into every corner, drinking from red plastic cups, laughing, flirting, screaming to one another over the music, spilling drinks all over what I'm sure are expensive couches and carpets.

It's like a scene from one of those John Hughes movies from the '80s that I've watched over and over with my dad. For once, I'm actually doing what everyone else my age is doing. It's awesomely cheesy and cliché and wonderful.

Charlie is high-fiving people as we make our way into the thick of things. Everyone seems to know and love him. And if they're wondering who the mystery girl is trailing behind, no one says anything about it.

Excitement fades into anxiety once we're in the middle of the party. My thoughts start to race. I am so clueless about how I'm supposed to navigate these people and their inevitable questions about where I've been hiding all these years.

Charlie seems to sense how uncomfortable I suddenly

am and puts a gentle hand on the small of my back. I relax and my brain stops its crazy whirring. Morgan, who misses absolutely nothing, ever, sees what's happening.

"I'm gonna...go do a lap. Or something. Away from you two," she says. Then she leans in, gives me a hug, and whispers in my ear, "I'm proud of you for being so brave—it took gigantic cojones to come to this party. And to reiterate what I told you yesterday: He really likes you. But just remember, if you need anything, flicker the lights and I'll burn this place down."

Morgan walks away, grabbing a red cup from a random guy and taking a swig as she goes. I wonder if there's any other option than beer here, which just the smell of makes me gag, and if I should push my luck by having some. The one and only time I drank before was at Morgan's house. Her parents went out, and we decided to do shots of crème de menthe, which is this weird mint-flavored liqueur. I ended up barfing, and I haven't been able to eat her mother's formerly awesome grasshopper pie since then. Apparently crème de menthe is the secret ingredient that makes it taste so good. Make that used to taste so good.

I stare up at Charlie. He stares back at me. We walk toward a table set up as a bar. Shyness washes over me like a tsunami.

"Morgan's hilarious," Charlie's saying over his shoulder. "How long have you guys been friends?"

"God, for as long as I can remember," I reply. "I mean, that's not true. I remember some things from before. Like fuzzy memories of being a toddler and eating an entire pad of paper while telling my doll it was a very, very bad thing to do. Ended up in the ER for that one. Also the time I was zoning out to *The Powerpuff Girls* while my mom was cooking dinner for me and I got a high-heeled Barbie doll shoe stuck up my nose. That was my second ER trip. Aaaaaaand I'm babbling again. Sorry. I babble when I'm nervous."

"So I've noticed." Charlie grins and hands me something pink and fruity-looking in a cup. I take a sip. It tastes a jillion times better than crème de menthe.

"Why are you nervous?"

I give him the simplified version. "I don't know anyone."

"Well, I know all these idiots, and you have nothing to be nervous about," he tells me.

"Come on now," I say. "You can't know *everyone*."

Charlie looks around the room before pointing discreetly at a loud, tall, red-faced boy doing shots. "See that guy?"

I nod.

"He pretends he's a dumb jock but he's in, like, every AP class. He's going to Yale, but he wants everyone to think he's a moron."

Yale. He wants people to think he's *not* going there? "That *is* moronic," I say. "I mean, it's Ivy League. The best of the best. I'd be wearing the sweatshirt to school every day. I'd love to go there."

"You should, then," Charlie says. "How could they pass up the valedictorian of your strict solo home school?"

I lean into him slightly. I love how warm but unyielding he feels. Soft yet strong. It's a nice combination.

"It's...complicated," I begin, thinking for all of a millisecond about telling him how college is not even a possibility because of my XP. I'm considering making a joke of it, saying maybe I could go to night school. But then something tells me not to ruin what is turning out to be a great night. There's enough time for reality later.

I nod over at a girl in a supertight, super-low-cut dress. "What about her?"

"Wore headgear to school until tenth grade, clearly trying to make up for lost time," he says, then motions to a short, acne-ridden boy. "Peed his pants on the sixth-grade field trip. And that girl over there, she has a prescription drug problem. Now see that dude? He has the longest fingers I've ever seen. He's also, like, one of the top ten cellists in the state. He's cool."

Charlie's saying this stuff like it's no big deal, but the whole time I'm thinking two things: (1) *I have missed out on so much*, and (2) *People never really outlive their pasts.* There will always and forever be the shorthand Headgear Girl and Wetpants Boy, and kids who graduated in this class will know immediately who that is, even at their fiftieth reunion. I decide to indefinitely postpone the conversation that will out me as Vampire Girl.

A guy jumps on Charlie's back out of nowhere. Charlie is startled and stiffens up like he's ready to throw down. Then a look of recognition crosses his face and he smiles instead.

"He's back!" the guy whoops. "Charlie's back! Why didn't you pregame with us? We had—"

Charlie's friend notices me standing there and stops talking. Another guy comes toward us trying to carry way too many drinks in way too few hands.

"Whoa, who's this?" the first guy says.

"Owen, Wes, meet Katie," Charlie says, gesturing to each boy as he makes the introductions so I can tell them apart.

Wes kisses my hand with wet, beery lips. "Katie, you're a magician. Teach us your ways," he says, giving me a deep bow.

I look at Charlie, then back at Wes. "What do you mean?"

"It means you got this guy to come to a party *and* make a smilelike feature. Our boy hasn't looked this good in a long time," Owen says, throwing an arm around Charlie.

We all start chatting and laughing like old pals, and it doesn't feel awkward in the least. But my newfound social comfort flies away when Zoe saunters over. Of course, she immediately starts hanging all over Charlie. "I'm sooooooo thirsty," she coos, staring up and batting her fake-feather eyelashes at him. I seriously don't understand how she doesn't just fly away. "Get me a drink?"

Charlie extracts himself from her grip and moves closer to me. "I can't right now; I've gotta give Katie the party tour."

Zoe plants herself in front of us so we can't move.

"Katie," she says, eyeing me suspiciously. "How come I've never seen you around before?"

"I—" I start to say, but Charlie jumps in before I can even begin to formulate some sort of lie.

"She's in the witness protection program," he says

with an easygoing charm. "If she told you that, she'd have to kill you."

Zoe gives him a little fake laugh, but she's still eyeing me. "On second thought, you actually *do* look familiar," she says. "Have we met somewhere before?"

I shake my head. "Don't think so."

She steps aside, her lips pressed together. "It'll come to me, don't you worry," she says.

Zoe glares at us as Charlie holds his hand out to me. I take it. I hope he can't feel how shaky the encounter with Zoe has left me.

"Ready?" he asks.

I follow behind him, leaving Zoe standing all alone and angry. I glance back at her over my shoulder as we head up the grand staircase, and she's still glowering at me like she wishes I'd self-combust. I'm sure she'd probably be thrilled to know it's an actual possibility in my case.

# 10

"And this," Charlie says, flipping the lights on in yet another room. This one is stacked floor to ceiling with antique-looking hardbound books. "Is the library."

"Ooooooooooh." I stare around with undisguised envy. "I would literally live in here if this was my house."

Charlie laughs. "I bet Zoe's never set foot in here, especially not to read."

His seemingly vast knowledge of her likes and dislikes, not to mention the floor plan of her house, unsettles me. My stomach churns with worry and fear. I wonder what kind of relationship Charlie and Zoe had or have and how he could ever like a girl like her when he also seems to like me. Zoe and I could not be more different in every possible way.

I swallow hard and turn to Charlie. "You seem to know Zoe pretty well," I say, trying to sound casual but feeling far from it. "And from what I could tell back in the living room, she seems to feel like she has some kind of a claim on you. So what's the deal with you two?"

Charlie puts his hands up like he's trying to deflect the question right back at me. "Whoa, where did that come from?"

I shrug. "I'm just saying, you're giving me a tour of her house like you live here. She looks at me like she wants to rip my head off because I'm with you. I just want to make sure I'm not getting in the middle of anything."

Charlie takes my hands in his and looks me straight in the eyes. "There's nothing to get in the middle of, I promise."

I stare back up at him, hungry for more explanation. There's more than nothing here. It's a definite something, or at least it was at some point. I raise an eyebrow like an unspoken question.

"Fine, we used to hook up once in a while," he finally admits. "Back when I was still Mr. Big Shot Swimmer. But it's not something I'm proud of or want to repeat or anything."

I nod. I appreciate his honesty even though I didn't really want to know that his lips have touched hers. I'm going to have a hard time getting that mental picture out of my head. The thought of those two together makes me shiver.

"You cold?" he says, noticing. "You can wear my sweatshirt if you want."

"No, I'm good," I tell him.

"And how about us? Are we good now?" he asks.

I think about it for a second. "Yeah. We're all good."

Charlie turns off the light and leads me back out into the long hallway. "You up for a game of beer pong?"

"I've never played," I admit. "But sure. Even though I hate beer."

And just like that, the tension over Zoe dissipates. "I'll show you how," he says. "In fact, I'll even drink the beer you're supposed to if you want."

"Sounds great," I tell him.

We head back into the den and watch the game already in progress. From what I can tell, beer pong consists of people taking turns chucking a little white ball into red cups set up in a triangle at either end of a table and then chugging the beer in them until it's all gone.

I'm not at all hopeful I'll be any good at it, but if Charlie's willing to down the drinks, I'm more than happy to give it a go. The players toss the ball and chug. Chug and toss. Eventually, that game ends and Charlie and I take on the winners.

He grabs the ball and mimics the throwing motion for me. "Just be gentle and get a good arc on it," he says. "It's a finesse game, not a brute force one. Go ahead. You got this."

He hands me the ball. I shoot. A flash of white curves through the air, then lands in the cup with a decisive little plop. I look up at Charlie in surprise. He high-fives me. The guy on the other side of the table chugs, then takes a shot. It misses.

"Go again," Charlie urges me.

Ball two of mine hits. Then three, four, five, and so on. I can't miss. The other team barely sinks any in our cups. Clearly, they are going to get very buzzed and Charlie will stay basically sober.

"She's a hustler! She's a beast! Where did she come from?!" Charlie whoops as I clinch the final toss.

I can't stop grinning. After years of being a failure at every sport I tried—I was serious about my dad being a terrible gym teacher—I've finally found one I'm good at. Beer pong. Too bad I can't tell Dad a thing about my newfound athletic prowess. I think he'd love the fact that I finally got to play a team sport after all these years, and earned all-star status at it, no less.

Morgan, who's been watching my quick ascent into the hall of fame from the sidelines, challenges us to the next game.

"Just you wait," Morgan trash talks from the other side of the table. "I've got a secret weapon on my team, too. He might not know how to tap a keg, but he definitely knows how to sink a Ping-Pong ball."

She slaps Garver on the back, trying to pump him up. Garver lobs it and sinks it on his first try. He turns and throws his arms around Morgan, jumping up and down and hugging her. She doesn't exactly return his enthusiasm. She peels his limbs from around her neck, puts some space between them, and gives him a fist bump instead.

"In your face!" Garver yells across the table at me. "Drink, Katie!"

"I got it," Charlie says as he reaches around and grabs the cup. "I'm a man of my word."

I take aim again and land the ball like the seasoned pro I am now. I'm on a total roll. I couldn't miss if I tried. Garver chugs.

His luck runs out on his next throw. The ball bounces off the rim of a cup, skitters to the ground, and rolls under the couch. Garver kneels down and goes to retrieve it.

"Dude!" Morgan complains to his butt crack, which is basically hanging out of his pants as he feels around under the couch. "You promised me you were good at this game!"

"I am good," he replies, reappearing and handing the ball to me. He pulls his pants back up. His butt crack disappears. "Just not as good as Katie."

It's my turn again. I hit their cups over and over. They miss more balls than they sink. I'd feel sorry for our opponents except that I'm having too much fun. I think I like parties. No, wait, I'm sure of it.

Before long, victory is ours. Again. Garver shakes Charlie's hand, flashes me a peace sign, takes a final gulp, and wipes the remaining foam from his lips. The beer has apparently given him extra courage, because he turns to Morgan and grins at her. "Do you wanna dance?"

Morgan scowls and gives him a death glare. "Garver,

what on earth makes you think I'd *ever* want to dance with you?"

I give her a look. She rolls her eyes at me. *Be nice*, I mouth at her.

"Fine," she says with a sigh. "Let's get it over with already."

Garver's face lights back up and he grabs Morgan by the hand. They weave through the crowd and join the mosh pit of kids bopping around the living room. I wonder if Morgan's thinking what I'm thinking right now: *We both missed out on a lot of fun not going to parties all these years.*

While I'm busy watching Morgan barely move and Garver jump around like a total spaz, I suddenly get the feeling people are watching *me*. I spy Zoe over in the corner whispering to a few other girls I sort of recognize from grade school. I have a hard time shaking the feeling that they are onto me. But then again, maybe they're just wondering who I am and where I came from; maybe some of them, like Zoe, feel as if Charlie is their property and don't like that he's with someone from outside their circle; or maybe I'm just imagining things. It's hard to tell.

"Is it me or is everyone looking at us?" I finally ask

him, nodding over at Zoe and her crew as discreetly as I can.

"They're not looking at us," he says. "They're looking at you."

He's looking at me, too, now.

There goes that intense heat up my cheeks again. "This is how I imagined all the middle school dances I never got to go to," I say, and it's probably pretty close: Zoe plotting revenge while I chat with the cutest guy in class, and her doing something heinous when I go to dance with him, like that scene in *Carrie* when she got pig blood spilled all over her at the prom.

"Well, it's not *quite* the same," Charlie replies with an easy laugh. He doesn't seem worried in the least bit about those girls, so I try not to be either. "At a middle school dance, all the girls would be on one side of the room and all the guys would be on the other and no one would touch."

I take a slow sip of my pink drink and stare up at Charlie over the top of the cup. "Oh, I'm pretty sure you danced with a *lot* of girls at middle school dances. Like Zoe and all her friends over there."

"Well, maybe. Though I wouldn't exactly call it dancing," he tells me. "It was more like the middle school grind."

"Eww," I say. I don't even want to think about any of

those mindless zombies grinding on Charlie. They don't deserve a great guy like him. "I'm pretty sure I don't want to know what that looked like."

"Actually, I think it's something you can't possibly miss out on," he says, taking the drink from my hand and putting it down on the nearest table. "Let's fill in some of those gaps in your homeschool education."

Charlie leads me out to the dance floor and spins me around. Then he brings me in so close there's almost no space left between us. I forget all about any potential pig-blood-spilling Zoe might be plotting.

I put my hands on Charlie's shoulders. He puts a hand on my lower back and starts swaying his hips side to side like a pendulum. I follow his moves. We burst out laughing.

"This is what you were missing!" Charlie crows.

"This is horrifying," I tell him, even though it isn't, not really. The actual dance might not be that great. But being this close to Charlie Reed definitely is.

"This move really worked for me!" he protests. "You don't like it?"

"I was hoping for a lot more twirling," I tell him. Hey, I'm actually flirting. It's actually working! Miracles do exist.

Charlie slowly spins me around. I make it a full 360 degrees without falling. It's possible I even look graceful. He pulls me back in and holds me close.

My heart is skittering around in my chest. I feel his beat back at mine in response. We're slow dancing in a sea of pogo people and I don't even care if we look silly for being so old-fashioned. I've never felt so perfectly connected to anyone or anything in my life except maybe my music. Zoe and her friends cease to exist in my mind.

Charlie looks at me, then down at my lips. *OhmyGod*, he's about to kiss me. He leans in. I inhale. Close my eyes. Wait.

And...Garver throws his arms around our necks. The moment is lost. I open my eyes back up.

"THIS IS THE BEST NIGHT OF MY LIFE!" Garver whoops, pointing at Morgan. He's sweaty and has beer breath and looks positively blissful. "SHE JUST KISSED ME!"

I stare over at my BFF. She shakes her head an emphatic no. But she's doing that thing she always does when she lies, twisting a chunk of hair around her finger. So maybe yes?

"If you ever say that again, I'll kill you!" she bellows. Garver grins and runs back over to her.

Morgan's still glaring at him, and I worry for a second that she's really going to punch him. But then he starts spaz dancing around her again and she starts cracking up. She watches his antics for a chorus or two, but after a while, it's like she can't help herself anymore. She starts dancing along with him. Garver looks like he's in heaven.

I turn back to Charlie. He leans in toward me again. Here comes that kiss. The one I've been waiting for my entire life. Finally. I want to remember every last detail of this moment forever and ever.

Except at the last second, I hear Zoe's voice in my ear instead of feeling Charlie's lips on mine. "I think I finally figured out where I know you from," she says, giving me a knowing smirk. "You weren't by any chance in Miss Eslinger's class in first grade, were you?"

The truth is, yes. We were both in that class. She must know it's me, Vampire Girl. I refuse to let her make me admit it, though. I'll tell Charlie about my XP when I'm ready, not because Zoe Freaking Carmichael is bullying me into it.

I shake my head and don't say anything. I can't. I'm worried my voice will betray how much I'm freaking out on the inside.

"Huh," she says, giving me an even closer look. "That's funny. Because you look just like this poor little girl in that class we used to call Vampire Girl. She got sick and never came back to school. I forget her name."

Before I can think of a way out of this, Charlie rolls his eyes at Zoe, then turns back to me and laughs. "So *that's* why you kept eyeing my neck out on the dance floor. And here I thought it was because you were so into me."

"What can I say? You're pretty irresistible, especially to us vampires." Even in my state of semipanic, I can't help but notice that his neck does look pretty awesome. *Smells good, too*, I think.

Zoe opens her mouth to say something else. But then her eyes register Charlie's arm draped over my shoulder and my hand stuck in his back pocket. She stomps away without another word. I can practically see steam coming from her ears.

"What the heck was that all about?" Charlie says.

I shrug. "Your ex-girlfriend is weird."

"She was never my girlfriend!" he protests before he notices my wide grin. "Oh. You're teasing me, huh?"

I giggle. "Maybe a little."

He starts leaning in toward me again. I hold my breath again. Close my eyes again. Wait again. Still no kiss.

This time his lips land next to my ear. "Do you wanna go somewhere?" he whispers.

I open my eyes, grin up at him, and nod. As if there's any answer but yes. I would go to the moon with Charlie Reed right now if he asked me to. We head out of the party to go make our own private one.

# 11

The nice thing about a small town is that you can get anywhere you want to go fairly quickly even if you are on foot: the train station, the ice cream shop where Morgan and Garver work, school (if you attend one outside your bedroom, that is), and, in this case, the marina. I have to hand it to Charlie—it's definitely the most romantic spot in all of Purdue.

The moon glints off the water as we stroll along the

dock hand in hand. Boats sway in the wind. Sails clang against masts. Stars sparkle overhead.

Charlie points at one of the boats. It's flying a blue flag with the iconic CAL written across it in gold script. "Fun fact: I was supposed to go to Berkeley on a swimming scholarship," he tells me.

Here's just the opening I've been waiting for. Now I can say, *Fun fact: I actually* am *that poor little girl Zoe was talking about before...*

But then I look into his eyes and see that he already seems to be bummed out enough without me adding to it. So instead, I say, "Supposed to? As in you're not going anymore?"

"Nope," he says. "I had to have surgery and they didn't know if I'd even be able to swim again. And no scholarship means no Berkeley."

I stare at my reflection rippling in the water and remember the Dear Gabby line about everyone having their own poop sandwich. Turns out she's right. Even Charlie Reed, the most perfect-seeming individual in the world, apparently has one. "Couldn't you get a loan or something?" I ask.

He shrugs. "Technically, I guess, but my dad's business

has been kinda shaky lately and I didn't want to put him under that pressure. Besides, swimming was, like, my whole life. I'm still trying to figure out who I am without it. So to waste my parents' money when I don't even know what I want to major in seemed pretty selfish."

"Wow, I'm really sorry to hear that." It's sad that Charlie lost his scholarship, but even sadder that he seems to think he's not worthy of a college education without swimming. "How did it happen? I mean, how did you get hurt?"

We keep walking and he doesn't respond for a good minute. I start to think he didn't hear me, but then he finally says, "A freak accident. I fell down some stairs and..."

He stops walking as he trails off. Then he turns to me, takes a deep breath, and starts over. "Actually, that's not at all true. That's just what I tell everyone. I was drunk at Owen's house and he bet me I couldn't jump off the roof into the pool and I clipped the edge and I'm an idiot."

"Wow" is all I can say at first. The version of Charlie that would do something so reckless doesn't fit with the one I'd imagined all those years, or the one I'm getting to know now.

"So, you're a *huge* idiot" is what comes out my mouth next, because apparently I don't want to be kissed by the guy I've dreamed about for years. I say it nicely, though, even as I shake my head in disapproval of both of us—him for being an idiot and me for also being an idiot. He's laughing, so I guess I haven't completely ruined my chances. "Thank you for telling me the truth," I say.

"Thank you for calling me an idiot." He smiles at me. "You know what the worst part is? I didn't even want to drink that night. It was so stupid—I don't want to be that guy, you know?"

"Then don't be," I tell him.

I know by the way he's acting that he doesn't normally let people see this side of him—the vulnerable part where he's not the king of the party, the king of the school, the king of the pool. It's probably easier with me, someone who's not a part of that whole scene. Still, I'm flattered he trusts me with his "stuff."

Which gets me to thinking: *I should probably share my stuff with him, too.* And he's just given me another perfect opening. But then Charlie breaks the silence before I get a chance to.

"I love it down here. Especially when nobody's around. It's the best at night," he says.

I decide to offer him something other than my diagnosis. It's still personal and close to my heart, but not quite as life altering as divulging my medical condition will be. "I remember my mom taking me here when I was little."

"Oh really?" Charlie sounds politely interested. He probably isn't prepared for what I'm about to say next.

"Yeah, I have this vivid memory of her letting me sit on her lap and showing me where to put my fingers on the guitar strings."

I take a breath as the mental picture washes over me full force. How can I miss someone so much who has been gone so long and who I had for such a short time to begin with? I touch the face of the watch I'm wearing, the one that was my mom's. It always makes me feel closer to her. I imagine she's somewhere up there among the stars now, light-years away, watching over me and keeping me safe.

"This was hers, actually," I add. "I spent so many days staring at this watch on her hand, hoping someday I could play like her. She died when I was six. Car accident."

Charlie goes silent. I hope I haven't scared him away, that he doesn't think I'm too damaged to get involved with. Because he doesn't even know about the sun damage yet. I am pretty much damage central.

"Wow, I...I'm really sorry," he finally says. "Here I

am talking about an injury that was all my fault. I really am a huge idiot."

I shake my head and smile up at him. "Not even. It's okay. I promise. It's nice to make a new memory here."

"Hey," he says, taking my hand. "Let me make it up to you."

I follow him down the dock until we stop in front of a gorgeous, gleaming yacht. It's like nothing I've ever seen before except possibly on TV, like maybe in a Kardashians' vacation episode. He climbs aboard and offers me a hand up. I join him on deck.

"This is yours?" I ask, my eyes as wide as the full moon. I don't get it. I thought he said his dad's business was shaky. This yacht must have cost them millions.

"Not mine," he replies, clearing that part up at least. "But I'm helping take care of it for the summer. It's my job. So now you know what keeps me busy during the day. Your turn."

I go for the easy joke, which isn't even a joke at all. "You haven't guessed by now? I actually *am* that little vampire girl Zoe was talking about before."

I wonder if I should make it clear that I'm actually not kidding. Just get everything out in the open. Before it's too late and I'm too invested and breaking the news has the potential for breaking my heart.

"I had a feeling," Charlie says. I'm pretty sure he has no idea I'm as serious as a heart attack, and at the last minute, I decide not to set him straight, at least not just yet. Maybe tomorrow. Not tonight. "But what the heck. I'll take my chances with you anyhow."

He takes me on a tour of the boat, pointing out different parts of it as we go. "This boat is a Jespersen. Kevlar-reinforced mainsail. Deck is Burmese teak with bamboo inlays."

I touch each of the components as he tells me about them. They reek of class and wealth. "None of that means anything to me, but it's so pretty!" I exclaim. "How do you know so much about boats?"

Charlie slings an arm around my shoulder, and I snuggle into him. "Remember that scholarship?"

I nod. The light of the stars and moon makes it look like he has a halo. Like he's my own personal angel.

"Well, they're kind of related," he explains. "The guy who owns this boat—Mr. Jones—is a Cal alum. Swam there just like I was supposed to. Once he found out about my scholarship, he kind of took me under his wing and taught me everything there is to know."

"That's nice," I murmur. "Having someone believe in you that much. Especially someone outside your family."

Charlie takes a big breath, then lets it out slowly. "Yeah. But it also sucks that much worse to disappoint someone like that. At least your family has to forgive you. I kind of feel like Mr. Jones hasn't looked at me the same since the accident. Good thing he still trusts me enough to do this job, though."

"I'm sure he doesn't think you're a disappointment—"

Charlie interrupts before I can finish the thought. "No, he definitely does. But it's okay, really. If I can't be in the water anymore, I at least like knowing I'll be on it regularly. This boat is the only place I can really think these days."

I wrap my fingers around Charlie's. "What do you think about when you're here?"

He stares up at the moon. "I don't know. What I'm gonna do now that the future I was supposed to have isn't going to happen. Where I want to go. Who I want to be. You know, minor things like that."

I laugh softly. "I completely and totally get it. I think about that kind of stuff all the time."

He looks at me, surprised. "You do?"

I smile up at him. "Yup. More than you can imagine."

"Huh," he says, digesting that piece of information. "You know what? One of these days we'll have to sail around the bay, watch the sun set..."

"That sounds perfect," I say, and it does. Too bad it's just a fantasy that can never happen. For now, though, I'm happy to revel in the unrealistic "someday."

Charlie's eyes meet mine again. And as if hanging out on a gorgeous boat, the night sky behind us, the water rocking us gently, isn't amazing enough, he leans in and kisses me. For real this time.

It is pure magic, so everything I ever hoped it would be, I can't even move or think or breathe for a second. But then instinct kicks in and I feel everything, everything. My nerve endings tingle, my brain is on fire, my heart is a goner.

I wrap my arms around his neck. He pulls me even closer. The kiss just keeps going and going.

And maybe it would never have ended, or at least not so soon, but the alarm on my watch interrupts us. It peals like church bells. We jump back from each other.

I push the off button and shake my head. Why oh why do I have such an early curfew? I barely ever go out; you'd think my dad could let me have a few extra hours when I actually do.

"You need to get home?" Charlie asks.

I lean my forehead against his chest. I can hear his heartbeat, clear and strong. It sounds like home. "Sometimes I hate this watch," I tell him even though I know it's not the watch's fault that I have an overprotective father, a mother who once wore it but can't anymore, and a rare disease that means I can't ever go on that sunset cruise with Charlie.

We walk back to Charlie's truck holding hands. He opens the door for me, and as I watch him walk around to his side, I decide that Real Life Charlie is even better than Daydream Charlie.

• • •

Charlie stops the truck about a block short of my house.

"What are you doing?"

"You said your dad was a light sleeper."

"It's nice of you to remember." I can't bear for this perfect night to end so I try to extend the conversation instead. "So when you're out on the boat doing all that thinking, do you ever come up with any good options for next year? Now that you're not going to Berkeley, I mean?"

Charlie nods, a smile creeping onto his face. "Well, first things first, I'm gonna buy a new truck."

My eyebrows furrow together. I was expecting to hear maybe a volunteer service trip, community college classes, an internship. Instead, he gave me a truck. That isn't a plan; it's a thing. "Why? This one is cool." It's one of those old ones—it looks like it belonged to a farmer once. I love it.

"Oh no, the new one is gonna be so much better," he explains, his eyes lighting up at the mere thought of it. "It'll have an extended cab with lift kits, chrome rims, matte finish."

"Sounds awesome," I say. "And expensive." I don't add: *And you're so much better than just wanting a truck. You should reach higher. You have so much potential.*

"Like I said before, you're not the only one who's really busy during the day," he replies with a shrug. "I've been busting my butt, so I should have enough money for it by the end of the summer. And then, I mean, I don't have any specific plan. Maybe I'll use my nice new wheels to drive cross-country. I've been in a pool my entire life, so I haven't gotten to see much else."

I nod. I know the feeling. I've never really been anywhere outside of Purdue.

"What are you doing—"

I cut Charlie off before he can get too specific in his questioning. I don't want to have to lie to him anymore, even by omission. Not after he's been so honest with me about his life.

"Me? I'm not doing anything. I mean, I'm not *going* anywhere." I know I'm talking too fast and kind of in circles. I hope he won't notice. "I'll take my online college classes, but basically I'll just be...*here*."

Charlie laughs. "That sounds great, but I was gonna ask you what you're doing *tomorrow*."

I fall back on the easy explanation. "Oh. Well. I'm busy during the day, but I'm free tomorrow night."

"Then I'll be right here," he tells me.

I lean over and give him a quick kiss on the cheek. Then I get out and start running toward my house. But something kicks in before I get there. Call it my conscience, or Jiminy Cricket, or an angel on my shoulder. Whatever it is gives me an urgent message: *He deserves the truth.*

So I turn around, walk back, and find Charlie still sitting where I left him. I take a deep breath. "I need to tell you something."

And I almost do it this time. Honestly I do. But then I

see his face, so earnest and open. He looks at me like I'm the totally normal girl I wish I actually was. And I just can't get myself to say the words.

"I've never owned a cat," I tell him instead.

Charlie laughs. "No shit."

# 12

The evening's events leave me dreamy and floating and inspired. I spend the rest of the night composing a new song—"Love Rocks"—that I honestly believe is the best thing I've ever written. It's complex, nuanced, and deep, an aesthetic I always strive for but haven't actually achieved until now. Or at least I hope I have. I drift off to sleep with a huge smile on my face just as the sun is starting to rise.

Morgan stops by after dinner. We're hanging out on my bed when I grab my guitar and start strumming. I value her opinion above almost anyone else's, so I want to hear what she thinks of my new song.

I'm singing my heart out, really getting into it. But when I look up to see if Morgan is feeling it along with me, I notice she's somewhere off in la-la land. She's smiling down at her phone, fingers flying across the keyboard.

I stop midsong and put down the guitar. "Who are you texting?"

She looks up, winces, then tosses her phone under the comforter. "What? No one. Sorry!"

"Morrrgannn," I say, elongating the syllables in an attempt to sound menacing.

She shrugs and mumbles something incoherent.

"What?"

More mumbles.

"I cannot hear a word you're saying. Can you speak up?"

"GARVER," she finally bellows. "I MADE OUT WITH GARVER."

I start smiling and can't stop.

"Shut. Up," Morgan growls.

"I didn't say anything!" I say, smiling even wider.

"Shut it."

I completely crack up. "I didn't say a word!"

Morgan turns beet red and pulls the blanket over her head. Through it, I hear, "He's kind of cute, though, right?"

"He's very cute," I assure her. "And sweet. And he obviously has good taste, because he's in love with you. I even liked his chili."

"We both know that last part's a lie. The chili was vile," Morgan says, her voice still muffled.

"Well, everything else I said was true."

As much as I'm loving the fact that Morgan is giving Garver a chance, I'm also worrying about how my dad is going to react to the fact that I have a date. Especially with a boy who has no idea about my XP. Dad will insist on meeting Charlie pronto. And when he does, he'll definitely let the cat out of the bag. And then the date—not to mention any relationship we might be headed toward—will be ruined. Charlie Reed already has enough on his plate without adding me and my weirdo disease to it. I can't deal with stopping this thing dead in its tracks before it ever gets a chance to really get going.

A plan is forming in my head, and I need Morgan's

help to carry it out. I decide since I was so successful at acting like a normal teen last night—hello, beer pong and stolen kisses on a boat that belongs to neither of us kissers—I should keep it going today and lie about my future whereabouts.

"Can I say I'm at your house tonight?" I ask Morgan. "I'm meeting Charlie later."

Morgan throws the blanket off her head and sits up. "You're asking me to help you lie to your father so you can spend time with a guy?" I swear, she's choking back tears, and Morgan never cries if she can help it. "I've never been so proud."

"You know what's weird?" I say, grinning back at her. "I'm kind of proud of myself, too."

"Go. Go do it now," she urges me, nudging me off the bed with her foot. "Before you lose your nerve."

I take a deep breath and head downstairs. I find my dad on the couch in the den sorting through photography portfolios. I feel awkward and weird, like he can see directly into my brain and already knows my plan.

"What are you working on?" I ask. It's a decent opener.

"Grading papers," he says as he holds a picture of a bird in flight up to the light. It looks pretty good to me. I'd give it an A.

"But you hate giving a letter value to a photograph," I say, repeating what my dad has told me a thousand times over. I'm working my way into the lie slowly.

"It's an impossible endeavor!" he tells me, putting down the photo and smiling. "So how was the party last night?"

"Good. Great!" I begin, then I backpedal. Better he thinks I wasn't enjoying myself so thoroughly. That will just lead to more questions, which will lead to more lies. "No, you know what, it was really boring. It was fine. It was nothing special."

My dad gives me a funny look. I try not to read anything into it. "Meet any fun people?" he asks.

"What—no. I mean, yes. Everyone was special," I stutter. "But no one was, like, *very* special. Everyone was equal. Which I guess makes them *not* special, technically—it was fun."

My dad raises an eyebrow but doesn't seem all that suspicious. I slap a big smile on my face and rush into my ask before my nerves get the best of me. "So anyway, do you mind if I go over to Morgan's tonight?"

He looks back down at his work and says nonchalantly, "Of course. No problem."

I grab my bag and head for the stairs before I can blow

it. "Great! I'll go tell Morgan. She wasn't sure you'd say yes, but I knew you would. You love Morgan! We all love Morgan! Okay then. Love you!"

"Love you more," my dad calls after me.

I would normally add *Not possible* here, like we always do. Instead, I turn around and head back into the den. "I'm lying."

He nods. "You were rambling, so I kinda knew."

I sit down next to him on the couch. "I'm going to meet a boy named Charlie Reed, whom you've never met, but he's really sweet and I know you'd like him and I really, really like him. A lot."

My dad's jaw clenches. I can't tell if he's angry or just worried. Probably both.

"Are you mad?" I ask softly.

"I'm not happy that you lied to me," he says.

A pit forms in my stomach. I hate disappointing my dad, who's basically given up his entire life for me.

"You know you can tell me anything," he adds.

"I know," I say, hanging my head. "I'm sorry."

"Thank you for telling me now, though," he says, relaxing a little. "So let me ask you something. Do you trust him?"

I nod. I completely and totally trust Charlie. I know I can from the way he remembered my dad was a light sleeper and stopped a block before my house when dropping me off. The way he ushered me through the party last night and didn't leave my side when he realized I was uncomfortable not knowing anyone. The way he made sure I didn't have to drink the beer in any of the games we played, and the way he looked at me before—and after—he kissed me. "One hundred percent yes."

A long pause. Then, "Will I hate him?"

I shake my head. "No, you really won't."

"And he knows about—"

I shake my head again. My dad's opening his mouth to object, so I start talking again before he can say anything.

"I haven't told him yet. But I will!"

"I'm not comfortable with him not knowing." My dad's voice is even firmer than before.

A big lump forms in my throat. I will not feel sorry for myself, not tonight, not when everything is going so well. "I'll tell him, Dad. I promise. I just need a little longer. Of being something more than just a disease."

"Oh, Katie," my dad says, looking like he's about to cry now, too. I know he wants to save me—from this disease, from potential heartbreak if Charlie walks away once I spill my secret, from my own mortality—and I also know, and he knows, too, that he's powerless in the face of it all. He wants to help his little girl and he can't. I imagine there could be nothing worse than that for a father.

I shrug, tears brimming in my eyes. My dad's jaw is set like stone. We stare at each other.

"You know you're more than that," he says.

"Not many other people do," I whisper, trying not to feel bitter. I am anyway.

He sighs and shakes his head. "You know I'm gonna need to meet him."

"You will, I promise. But in a few days. Like a normal girl, right?"

I wait. I pray silently he'll agree. Finally he nods. I throw my arms around his neck.

Just then, Morgan walks downstairs. She gives my dad a casual smile, and says, "Hey, Mr. P, is it okay if Katie and I hang out together the entire night?" She's one hundred percent convincing. I clearly need to take lying lessons from her.

"I admitted everything," I tell her.

"Are you serious?" She looks down at her watch. "You couldn't last ten minutes?"

I shrug. "What can I say? I'm a good kid to the core. I'm new at this kind of thing."

"You're hopeless, Katie," she says, shaking her head. "Have fun tonight. I gotta go to work now."

# 13

"So, where to?" Charlie asks when I jump in his truck a few hours later.

I can see now why he's saving for a new one. The odometer in here registers more than 150,000 miles, the fabric seats are practically worn through, and the engine makes a little chugging noise that's definitely not supposed to be there.

"Let's go into town," I suggest. Morgan and I came up

with a great plan before she left. I think Charlie's going to love it.

Charlie grins. "Your wish is my command."

He hits the gas. *Chugachuga-chugachuga.* We're off.

Tiny little Purdue is practically deserted even though it's only nine forty-five by the time Charlie pulls into a parking spot. Charlie and I stroll along Main Street, looking in windows and chatting about our days.

When we get to the ice cream shop, I stop short. "Well, here we are."

"Looks like we're too late," Charlie says. "They're closed."

"Oh, ye of little faith," I say.

I peer in the window and wave Morgan over. She and Garver are the only people inside; all the customers have long since gone home.

"Oh, strange," Morgan says in a stilted tone as she holds the door open for us. "I didn't see anyone sneak in after hours, I swear, Mr. Bossman!"

"Me neither," Garver says from behind the counter.

Charlie gives me a look. "Ooooh, you're smooth, Katie."

"Now don't screw us over, friends," Morgan says, handing me the keys as we step inside. "Make sure to clean up, turn off the lights, and lock up when you leave."

"You got it," I assure her.

"I'll come by and grab the keys in the morning," she says, and then leans in to me, and whispers, "Have fun. Maybe even too much."

"You, too," I say, gesturing toward Garver.

"Not a word," she says to me, then she heads for the door. "Garver, you coming?"

"No doubt." He gives Charlie a light punch on his arm as he heads for Morgan and they walk out of the shop.

And then we're alone again. All the chairs are turned over on the tops of the tables, so we head to the counter. Charlie plops himself down on a stool while I put on an apron and the dorky little paper cap the employees here have to wear.

"What'll it be, sir?" I say, getting into character.

"Double banana split, hot fudge, whipped cream, nuts, the works," Charlie tells me.

"Eww," I say, not making a move toward the cartons of ice cream or toppings. "Nuts. No. They do not go with ice cream. Everyone knows that."

Charlie pretends to be outraged. "What happened to the customer is always right?"

"You kissed that good-bye when you mentioned nuts."

"Nuts," he says, snapping his fingers.

"Tough break," I tell him.

He leans forward until his forehead is touching mine. I sink into his eyes. He softly kisses me. He adds just the right amount of lips, tongue, and time. The kiss is perfect, just like Charlie.

We pull back and stare at each other. A huge smile creeps up my lips as I pick up the ice cream scoop and grab a big bowl for the two of us to share. Who knew having a crush could feel this great? I've spent so many years of my life alone in my room. What a waste. "Now back to the subject at hand," I say. "We've already established nuts are out. Can we negotiate the banana portion, too?"

Charlie shakes his head. "Not a big fan of potassium either, huh? What is with you?"

I shrug. "I just think bananas are gross. Besides, the ones imported from Central and South America can have these huge hairy spiders hiding in them. Like, ones as big as your palm!"

"Pretty sure that's an urban legend," he tells me.

"Nope, I've done my research. See, banana trees have these tightly coiled leaves going up, and then the banana flower leans down over that," I explain, using my hands to show how the plant grows. "So it's the absolute perfect place for spiders to live. One kind, called the wandering spider—it's from the Ctenidae family—like, rears up on its back legs and opens its fangs when it's threatened."

"Kind of like this," Charlie says, acting it out. *"RAWW-WWRRRR!"*

I laugh. "Pretty much. Good impression. Except I'm pretty sure spiders don't roar. In fact, I'd hazard a guess they don't make any sound at all."

"Minor details," he says. Charlie's lips are pressed together and his eyes are dancing. He's trying not to laugh at me. He's just barely succeeding.

"What?" I ask him.

"You're just so cute," he says. "And smart. How do you know everything?"

I remember too late Morgan's telling me to avoid spouting all my nerdy knowledge around Charlie. But I can't help it. I love facts and science and nature and the stars and skies and infinity and beyond. I love it all. I want to know it all.

"I don't know everything. Not by a long shot," I say, digging into the cookie dough ice cream. "Not yet, at least. Though I'd like to. It's an unachievable goal, but I still think it's a good one."

"Well, you know a lot," he says. "I mean, you just graduated high school and already you have a ton of college credits. I just graduated high school and...I know how to swim and fix boats, and that's about it."

I plop a scoop of toffee bar crunch next to the chocolate chip cookie dough one, then add another of salted caramel pretzel. Grabbing a can of whipped cream and two spoons, I set everything down on the counter between us.

"Look, you're only eighteen. You're not supposed to know everything yet," I tell him, squirting a huge dollop of whipped cream on top of each scoop. Our dessert looks like a fairy-tale castle now. "Or ever, really. Learning is lifelong, you know?"

"I guess I just worry sometimes that my best days are behind me," he says, dipping his spoon into the cookie dough scoop and then licking it thoughtfully. "I mean, from where I'm standing now, it's like I can't see two feet into my future. I've honestly never felt so unfocused in my life. Is that weird?"

"Weird? No. Human? Yes," I tell him. "And what do you mean, your best days are behind you? Your life is just starting. It can be whatever you decide to make it."

He digs into the salted caramel and sighs. "I guess it's just that this huge part of my life ended, you know? And it's what everyone knew me for at school. All my friends were swim-team guys. I trained for it every day. It's what made me who I am... or, I guess, who I was. And now I'm not that guy anymore, and I can't figure out where or how I fit in."

I can oddly relate to what he's saying. What would my life be like if I wasn't the girl with the rare and life-threatening disease? It would certainly be different, and I might not know where I belonged either. But I *am* the girl with the disease. Kind of like how Charlie's now the guy with the injury. "Do you feel like people treat you differently since your accident?"

He nods. "I know you'd probably rather not hear any more about her, but take Zoe Carmichael, for example. Her party was the first night she's even talked to me since I got hurt, and I'm sure that's only because she saw me with you. Zoe's the kind of girl who doesn't like sharing her toys even if she's already decided she doesn't want to play with them anymore."

"Seems like an accurate assessment," I say. "So, like... you think she used you for your social standing or something like that? And then ditched you when you weren't in the papers or breaking records every week anymore?"

"Yeah, something like that," he replies with a nod. Then a weird look crosses his face. "Hey, how did you know I was in the paper and broke swimming records?"

*You have to be more careful*, I silently chide myself. *You just almost outed yourself as his creepy lifelong stalker.* "We valedictorians are known to have excellent research skills," I tell him.

He grins at me. "So you googled me, huh?"

I shrug. "*Mais oui.* I have to know what I'm getting into, right?"

And then I plant my lips on his. They taste like sugar and cream and pure goodness. This kiss lasts much longer than the first one. I've never felt so buzzed on life.

When it finally ends, he says, "You know what tonight reminds me of? *Sixteen Candles*. Like that scene at the end, where Sam and Jake kiss over her birthday cake?"

I nod. He has no idea how perfect what he just said to me is. It's my most favorite movie ever, and I've been wishing to get a kiss as special as that since the first time Morgan and I watched it. And now here comes Charlie, making all my dreams come true.

"I've always thought it would be cool to have

something like that but in real life. And now I do," he says, heading back in for another kiss.

So maybe I'm making some of his dreams come true, too.

• • •

Every night that week starts and ends in much the same way: I convince my dad to give me just one more night as a normal girl, and he reluctantly agrees. I jump in Charlie's truck and off we go on another adventure. Bowling one night, window-shopping the next (because, of course, the stores are closed), to the late movie at the mall a few towns over from Purdue.

We talk, we laugh, we kiss. A lot. He drops me off, but not before asking me out for the next night. I always tell him I'm free only in the evening, a response he accepts, no questions asked. It's an idyllic existence, one I never thought I'd get a chance to experience. I think this is how my parents must have felt when they first met: young, free, and incredibly happy.

Things are so perfect, I even start to delude myself that maybe I never have to tell Charlie. My dad, however, disagrees.

"This is the last time I'm going to say yes, Katie," he

tells me, his mouth set in a straight line as I'm leaning hard on my "please just let me be normal a little longer" speech. "After tonight, I am meeting this young man. I need to know him. And he needs to know about your XP."

His words hit me with a thud. More than anything, I do not want the magic to end. And telling the guy I seriously think I might be falling in love with that things aren't exactly what I've led him to believe they are will be the equivalent of pulling the curtain back and seeing that the great and powerful Oz is just some guy with a microphone and a Napoleon complex. Everything will change.

"Okay, Dad," I say, wishing there was some other way and knowing there isn't, not really. "Tomorrow, you meet Charlie and then I will tell him about my situation. Tonight I'm still a regular girl."

My dad smiles at me, but the fine lines around his eyes are suddenly looking more pronounced and prolific. I don't want to be the cause of his premature aging. But the heart wants what it wants. I couldn't stop now if I tried.

• • •

Charlie and I head to the beach this time. It's quiet and we're the only ones around. Charlie gathers some sticks and leaves, puts them in a pile inside a circle of rocks someone else already made, and lights a little bonfire.

We're sitting on a blanket. I'm snuggling into him, resting my head on his shoulder. He's tracing lazy circles on my back. Everything about "us" just feels so right: The way we can talk about everything or nothing at all and it's never awkward. The way our hands fit together like two pieces of a puzzle. How we never seem to get annoyed or sick of each other.

Charlie points to a star. By now, he knows all about my obsession with the constellations and how I want to be an astrophysicist someday. "So which one is that?"

"That one's called Altair," I tell him. "I think it's sixteen light-years away. So the light we're seeing was actually created when we were, like, two years old."

"That's insane." Charlie laughs and points to another. "What about that one?"

"That's Sirius."

"Like the radio?"

I give him a playful nudge with my elbow. "It's the dog star. Almost nine light-years away."

Charlie gets quiet. I can almost hear the gears turning in his mind. For a brief second, my heart quickens as I wonder if he's somehow found me out. Even though

I know how unlikely it is, I can't help thinking about all the ways it could happen. Maybe Zoe's been doing some sleuthing and texting him her discoveries? Telling him about my disease is going to be hard enough. Maybe she found our class photo from kindergarten and has managed to identify me even though none of our names were on that photo and I had a weird bowl cut that year. (I guess it's lucky I left school so early in first grade that I missed photo day.) Having him hear about it from someone other than me would be devastating. I feel like it would break any trust we've built up in the short time we've known each other. I have to tell him. I have to. I gather my courage.

"What are you thinking about?" I ask, holding my breath.

He hesitates. I can tell that whatever he has to say is something big and weighing heavily on him. "The coach at Berkeley called me the other night. I guess one of the other swimmers transferred, so a spot just opened up."

I exhale. "Are you serious? You could get your spot back?"

I am deliriously happy for him. Because if there's anyone who deserves a lucky break and a shot at college, it's Charlie Reed. He's smart and sweet and thoughtful and hardworking and all sorts of other good things. I'm so glad the universe is recognizing that one mistake shouldn't have to mean all his dreams die with it.

Charlie shrugs. "I mean, technically, yeah. There's a meet coming up in a month, and the Berkeley coach will be there. I'd have to get back in shape by then, which is probably impossible, and then make, like, the best time ever to prove I'm fully rehabbed."

I grab him by his shoulders. "You could totally do it. I know you could."

Charlie stares into the fire like he's going to find the meaning of life in its flames. "I don't know. I might have some reasons to stick around here next year…"

It's maybe the sweetest thing anyone has ever said to me. "I'll be right here when you come home to visit. Promise."

My phone's been buzzing like crazy in my pocket all night, and I've been ignoring it. But it's getting late and I know I should've been home hours ago, a fact my dad is probably reminding me of at this very second. I sigh and check out my texts. There are five from my dad and twenty-five from Morgan.

"Oh shit," I say under my breath.

"Everything okay?" Charlie asks. "Oh, wow, it's late. Like, really late. We gotta get you home before your dad flips."

"Yeah," I say, not moving.

I scroll through Morgan's messages. Each is more panicked than the last. I flip from worried that my dad is going to never let me out of the house again to being annoyed. She's not my mother; she's my best friend. If I'm staying out late with Charlie, she's supposed to be cheering me on, not telling me to go home.

**Where are you?**

**You were supposed to be home by eleven.**

**Your dad is pretending to not freak out. But he totally is. I know because he texted me to see if I know where you are.**

**One o'clock now. Helllloooooooo, earth to Katie.**

**It's two am. Do you know where your best friend is? I don't.**

**Three in the morning. Still no word from you.**

**OK NOW I AM FREAKING OUT.**

**ARE YOU DEAD? PLEASE REPLY YES OR NO.**

**SUNRISE IS IN TWO HOURS... YOU ARE CUTTING IT WAY TOO CLOSE, KATIE.**

Morgan's been staying out just as late these days with Garver, so I don't know why she's being so intense with me. I am fully aware that I need to get home soon. How stupid does she think I am?

"What's up?" Charlie asks.

"Nothing, really," I say, a thought occurring to me. "Morgan's just not used to sharing me with anyone, I guess. I think it's hard for her that I'm spending so much time with you. I'll make sure I spend some quality time with her tomorrow so she doesn't feel so neglected."

"Girls," Charlie says, rolling his eyes. "Although I guess they're not *all* bad."

"There are a couple decent ones."

Charlie stands, brushes the sand off himself, and offers me a hand up. "I wish we could just, like, sleep out here. It'd be pretty cool to wake up with you in my arms instead of my ratty old teddy bear."

I love the idea of waking up next to Charlie. I love the image of Charlie hugging his childhood stuffed animal almost as much. "Someday before you . . . go do whatever it is you decide to do in the fall, we'll have to make that happen," I tell him.

"Deal," he says. "Time to get you home. And then tomorrow I'm gonna take you on a real date, okay?"

I nod and drop the bomb on him. "That's perfect. 'Cause you need to meet my dad."

# 14

Charlie drops me off, I walk through the door, and Dad's right there to greet me. His hair is standing straight up like he's been running nervous fingers through it all night. His eyes are hollow and haggard. He throws his arms around me and hugs me so tightly I can't breathe.

"Sorry I'm late," I say into his shoulder.

He pulls back and gives me a long, hard look. "Don't you ever scare me like that again, Katie! I thought you were dead. I have no idea who this boy is or what he thinks he's doing keeping you out until all hours of the night—"

"This wasn't Charlie's fault. Breaking curfew is all on me."

"If you were any later, you could've gotten UV exposure!" Dad says, getting angry now that he can see I'm alive and well. "You should know better than anyone what that kind of trigger can lead to!" He's so worked up now, he's practically spitting the words out.

"Dad, chill," I say. "Look at me. I'm fine. No harm, no foul."

"Only because you were lucky this time," he says.

I heave a huge sigh. I truly can't take being coddled one second longer. "Dad! Listen to me. I'm not a child. I can take care of myself. I can make my own decisions. I'm sorry that tonight I chose to stay out later than you were comfortable with, but I'm fine." My voice rises with my frustration level. "No, I'm more than fine. I'm the happiest I've ever been in my life. Can't you see that?"

He shakes his head sadly. "All I can see is my little girl ready to throw away everything we've worked so hard for on a boy who doesn't respect our house rules."

"Will you stop judging Charlie? You don't even know him!" I yell. "He's the best, most kind, and most respectful boy I've ever met! The only person you have a problem with here is me. Your own daughter. If you hadn't noticed, I've grown up, Dad. I'm not a little girl who can be satisfied with you blowing up photos you took on safari and creating a fake African savannah for me in the basement anymore. I need to get out and really live."

My dad looks ready to cry. I'm so aggravated now, I might, too. I can't believe my night turned on a dime like this, from perfect to total disaster in a matter of minutes.

"I knew this might happen once you got to a certain age," my dad says, almost to himself. "You're so strong-willed. I guess it's inevitable that would work against me."

I step forward, put my arms around his neck, and rest my head on his shoulder. "Dad, I'm fine. I promise. In fact, I'm more than fine. I'm great. Maybe for the first time since I got diagnosed. Please just let me be normal. Please. You have to trust me."

He relaxes into the hug. "I just want you to be safe, Peanut," he says. "You're my girl. I can't bear to think of anything bad happening to you."

"I know," I tell him. "I love you. I promise to text next time I'm going to be late. And I promise you're going to love Charlie when you meet him. He's coming to pick me up tomorrow—well, tonight, I guess. And he can't wait to meet you." So I might be exaggerating a little... "He's a good guy, Dad. He reminds me of you."

"I hope you're right," he says. "I hope he takes the news about your XP like the respectful, mature young man you say he is. I hope he doesn't run away because he can't handle it."

I hate that my dad thinks Charlie might ditch me when he finds out about my disease. So much so that I tell him the biggest lie of my life. It's a whopper. "He already knows," I say. "And it doesn't change the way he feels about me in the least bit."

Dad's wrinkles relax. He truly seems happy for me. "That's great," he tells me. "Really. It's everything I've ever wished for you."

I feel bad about making up Charlie's reaction, but not bad enough to take back what I've said. I'm fairly certain it will become the truth once I finally get up the guts to actually tell him anyhow.

I text Morgan once I'm back in my room. **I'm home. Safe and sound.**

She texts back: . . .

**Don't be mad--my dad isn't.**

Three bubbles appear, then disappear. There they are again. There they go. Finally, a text comes through. Another ellipsis.

I don't think I can remember Morgan ever getting mad at me before.

**I know you're used to being my only contact to the outside world. But at least try to be happy for me, please.**

More bubbles popping up and then leaving. Then this. **Are you kidding me? I am not jealous of your stupid boyfriend. Good for you! All I'm trying to do is make sure you're alive to actually enjoy your relationship with Charlie. Sorry for caring.**

**Doth the lady protest too much? Methinks yes,** I type. I'm not actually going to send it, but then I hit send by mistake and it goes flying out into the world.

Morgan's reply comes quickly. **Get over yourself. And don't come crying to me when he turns out to be an ass about your XP. Not everyone is as cool as me about stuff like that.**

Ugh. First my dad and now Morgan assuming that Charlie will leave me when he finds out. I re-create my lie and decide it only counts as one since it's the same thing I told my dad.

Charlie is. He knows and he's completely cool.

Good for him. Good for you. I'm turning off my phone and going to sleep now. I was up all night. Later.

Who knew relationships could be so complicated? I toss and turn in bed, worrying about how to convince my dad to give me more freedom. How to actually tell Charlie what I supposedly already told him. What to do about Morgan. I'm mad at her, but maybe I shouldn't be. Maybe I should apologize to her, not the other way around.

Eventually, I fall into a fitful sleep.

# 15

"So tonight's the night," my dad says.

"Yup," I say, gnawing on a nail. I know I shouldn't be this nervous. How could my dad not like Charlie? He's, like, perfect. Not to mention a perfect gentleman. Still, there's a lot riding on what my dad thinks of him. I need everything to go just right.

"But you're going to be normal, right?" I've managed to convince my dad to not lecture Charlie about XP and how dangerous it was for me to be out so late last night. I've told him that normal dads don't talk about their daughters' medical conditions when they meet the Boyfriend.

This one lie sure is snowballing. And it does not feel good. My life as a rebellious teen is really stressing me out.

The doorbell rings. I let Dad answer it alone. The plan is that I'm supposed to go to my room and wait until he calls for me, but I can't stand the suspense of not knowing how it's going. I walk halfway up the stairs and stay put.

I hear Charlie introducing himself, my father ushering him into the den, then telling him to sit.

"Ever been arrested?"

This is my dad's idea of an opening line? I can't even.

"No, sir," Charlie replies.

Dad's questions come rapid fire and only go downhill from there. "What's your curfew?"

"One AM."

"What time do you actually get home?"

"Around two," Charlie admits. "Sometimes later. Like last night. I'd like to apologize to you, sir, for getting Katie home so late. We lost track of time."

"Don't do it again," my dad tells him. "Now, why aren't you going to college?"

Ugh. I'm sure Charlie didn't want me discussing with my father how I think he should use the money to fund his education instead of tooling around the country in a new truck. The little nest egg he's accumulated would probably cover classes at the community college and then some. After that, he could transfer to UW and still afford it with in-state tuition and maybe some loans and grants. (I may have done a little research on this in preparation for subtly suggesting it to Charlie.)

"I got hurt and lost my swimming scholarship," Charlie tells him. I wonder if he's looking my dad straight in the eyes or staring at his feet like he does when he's sad and/or uncomfortable.

"How many times a week do you shave?"

"Like four...?" I can hear the confusion in Charlie's voice. He's definitely thinking *Why does it matter?*

"I don't believe you," my dad tells him. I'm dying. What is this, the Inquisition? Who cares how many times a week he shaves? "Who's your team?"

"The Seahawks," Charlie answers. This *has* to win my dad over.

But my dad persists. "Why?"

Charlie gets bonus points here. "Because they're great and also because one time I met Richard Sherman at this burger place and he ate some of my fries."

There's silence for a good minute. I'm sure Charlie is squirming in his seat. I know I am. I'm desperate to go save him. I keep staring at my phone, waiting for that text to pop up telling me I can go join them.

Finally, my dad cracks. "That's awesome. That's important."

I know he's grinning. I'm so happy. Until a second later when he almost outs me. "Charlie, I know she seems strong, but she's fragile. She—"

I'm not waiting for any text; I go bounding down the stairs, yelling a greeting that's really meant to interrupt the bomb-dropping in progress. "Hey! What are you guys talking about?"

Charlie gets up from the couch to give me a hug.

"Nothing, just getting to know each other," my dad says.

"Wow," Charlie says.

He's staring at me like he can't believe I exist. It's funny because it's not like I'm dressed up or anything. I'm wearing jeans and a T-shirt and weathered white Vans. But I did do my hair and makeup just like Morgan showed me, so maybe that's it.

I reward him with a huge smile, grab my guitar case

from where it's sitting in the corner—Charlie told me to bring it, I don't know why, but he sounded so excited I couldn't say no—and give my dad a little hug.

"Well," Dad says, "be safe, okay?"

I nod. "Love you as much as possible."

Charlie reaches out his hand. They shake. "Thanks for letting me take her out, Mr. Price," he says. "I'll take good care of her."

We're about to walk out the door when my dad calls after us. "Wait! Let me take your photo."

I whirl around, embarrassed. "Dad..."

But Charlie seems perfectly happy to oblige my father's mortifying whims. He puts his arms around me from behind. "What do you think, prom pose?"

I laugh. My dad raises the camera to his eye. "Ready?"

I look up at Charlie and he looks down at me. We're grinning at each other. No phony smiles for us. The flash goes off, and we're on our way.

# 16

"The train station?" I say as Charlie pulls into a space in the parking lot.

I'm trying not to look disappointed—I don't know what I expected for our date.

"You might know where we are, but do you know *why* we're here?" he asks, pulling me along by the hand.

I shake my head. "No, but I hope you're not trying to make me play on the platform tonight. Remember how awkward that got the first time around?"

Charlie laughs. "How could I forget the dead-cat funeral you had to go plan? It is where we first met, though."

He has a point. And I start to feel the disappointment slip away.

We stop short right in front of Fred's little window. There are two tickets waiting there for us.

"I believe these are yours," Fred says, grinning at me.

I look from Charlie to Fred and then back to Charlie again. "Where are we going? And why do I have my guitar?"

Charlie shrugs and smiles. I try Fred. He gives me an even more exaggerated shrug.

"I know nothing," Fred tells me.

"Fred…" I try to implore him to spill it with the most innocent and sweetest look I can muster.

"Don't even try it," he tells me, pretending to lock his lips and throw away the key. "I'm a steel trap."

The train is approaching. Taking us on an adventure to who knows where. I'm so excited.

The doors open and the conductor gives me a huge smile. We've exchanged hellos before when I was playing here, but he's certainly never had me as a passenger. "All aboard," he calls out.

Charlie and I climb the stairs and head into a car. It's basically deserted. Just us, dim lighting, and the rumble of the tracks underneath the wheels.

"Your seat, mademoiselle," Charlie says, gesturing to an empty row.

I put my guitar down in the aisle and slide in. Charlie sits across from me. He starts setting up paper plates, napkins, and plastic silverware on the table between us.

"I slaved all day on this," he says, reaching into his backpack and pulling out a big bag from my favorite Chinese food place. I shake my head in disbelief when I realize all the trouble he went through to make tonight perfect for me. He's included all my favorites: lo mein, orange chicken, fried rice.

"Did you just pull Chinese food out of your backpack?" I laugh. "Do you always travel with hot food?"

"This is a romantic picnic!" Charlie exclaims, trying to keep a serious look on his face and totally not succeeding. "You can't ride a train without Chinese food out of a backpack."

"I don't know, that could be true, I've never been on a train before," I say.

"Neither have I," Charlie tells me.

"Really?" I thought I was probably the only person on earth who hasn't. I love that it's the first time for both of us. We "clink" our chopsticks and dig in.

"You know what I've been thinking about?" he says when we're almost done eating. "How insane it is that you've lived right here since you were little and I've never seen you riding your bike or, like, out with a lemonade stand. I would have bought your lemonade!"

My heart skips a beat. The last thing I want to discuss right now is why we never met until a few weeks ago. I just want to enjoy the dinner, the ride, the date. Keep things light while we still can. I promise myself that I'll tell him before the night is over.

When he drops me off tonight, before he gets out to walk me to the door (like I know he will), I'll come right out and say it. I'll be factual and to the point. No drama. "I hope this doesn't change anything between us," I'll say. Easy-peasy, just like that.

When I imagine it this way, I can't imagine Charlie, like, screaming and running away or rejecting me or never talking to me again. I really don't think my worst fears will come true. He's too good of a person to freak out over some faulty DNA. And he'll understand why I didn't tell him. I know he will.

For now, though, I tell him, "I don't like lemonade," as if that covers it.

He presses his lips together and gives me a look. "You do know I know the truth, right?"

I'm about to apologize for not telling him myself when he leans forward and looks left, then right, then directly at me again. "You're an international spy. You were always off on missions in exotic locations while I was sitting in the cafeteria, bored out of my mind. I'm sure Katie Price isn't even your real name," he whispers.

I'm relieved that he was only kidding around, but I feel like it's one close call after another. Maybe my news can't wait until the end of the night. Might as well rip this Band-Aid off now—as quickly as possible—and just deal with whatever happens as a result. Reality is reality; I can't change what is. "That's very close. The real truth is..."

But I start rethinking how he'll take the news now that I'm about to be faced with it. All my confidence that he'll be chill and cool and that nothing will change is gone. I decide he'll probably *pretend* it doesn't matter and profess that my condition won't come between us. But then we'll somehow start seeing less of each other. He'll suddenly become busy at night. And the best thing that's ever happened to me will be over.

I lean my elbows on the table and decide to offer up half the story. Test the waters. "No exotic locations. Because you're my mission. I was under strict orders not to be seen, but I've been watching you for years from the safety of my own room."

A beat. Charlie blinks. Then he grins at me. "See? I was close. Sorry if I blew your cover."

He gathers up the now-empty boxes of Chinese food and goes to throw them out. When he comes back, he slides into the seat next to me and puts his arm over my shoulders. We watch the stars go by as the train chugs along.

"You were so young. When your mom died, I mean," he says softly.

"Yeah." I often wonder about what happened to my mom after the car hit her. What did she think about? Was there a white light, did her grandparents escort her to heaven? Will she get me when it's my turn? Or will it just be blackness, a big void, a curtain coming down and that's it, like I never existed at all? For some reason, I always get stuck on that last thought. It's, like, my biggest fear, even though I can't explain why. I *have* to make a mark on this world before I'm forced to leave it. I *have* to make my time here matter somehow.

"That must've been awful," Charlie says, interrupting

my dark and desperate thoughts. "Do you remember much about that time?"

I think back for a moment. Dad and I dealt with Mom being gone in much the same way we're dealing with the current situation: We slap a smile on our faces and power through, usually pretending the problem doesn't exist at all. Like if we ignore it long enough, maybe it'll just go away.

"Um, honestly, all I remember from that time is my dad. Watching him pretend to be okay so I'd be okay. And I'm pretending to be okay so he'll be okay," I tell Charlie. "But somehow … you know, I guess we actually did make each other okay. We learned how to miss her together without being swallowed by the grief."

Charlie nods. "Yeah, you and your dad seem like you're really close."

I shrug, staring out the window at Cassiopeia. According to Greek mythology, she's chained to a throne, forever stuck there as punishment for her boastfulness and vanity. I wonder sometimes if I did something to deserve XP, something terrible that requires me to do penance in my house and my room all day, every day, until the sun sets.

"Yeah. I wish he knew me a little less well, though," I say.

This isn't an entirely true statement. I know I'm lucky my dad loves and understands me. I just wish I had an opportunity to be loved and understood that same way by more people, people my own age, like, at college. I want to be heading off in the fall, too, instead of watching everyone else's lives expand while mine continues to contract. I'm terminally frustrated by my situation, especially by the recent realization that having XP basically means neither of the people closest to me will ever consider me an adult in the same way they would if I was disease free. They'll always feel the need to watch over me and baby me.

"Ready for dessert?" Charlie asks.

I nod.

"Okay then. Hold out your hand and close your eyes," he commands.

Charlie pours a pile of something into my cupped palm. "You can open up now."

I stare down at my hand. In it is a pile of Skittles, like the ones he kept trying to return to me the first night we met. I smile up at Charlie.

"I got moves for days," he says. "Hey! We're almost here!"

I look out the window and see the Seattle skyline

coming into view. I don't know where I thought we were going, but this is even cooler than I ever could have imagined.

"Seattle?! Cool!"

The train comes to a stop and we get off. Neither of us really knows where we're going, and I'm pretty sure Charlie's agenda was just *Let's hit Seattle and figure it out when we get there.* We find ourselves wandering along the waterfront. Everything about being here is new and exciting, and it's honestly enough for me to just be looking at the glittery span of parks and piers that seems to go on forever.

I gape at all the sidewalk cafés dotting streets that wind around in a seemingly endless maze. Despite its being after what I would assume is most kids' bedtimes, there are a lot of them still out eating with their parents. Guys with tight pants and hipster facial hair peck away at their laptops in coffee shop windows. Couples out on dates toast with glasses of champagne.

But what really blows my mind is how many people are out performing in the streets. Back in Purdue, I was always the only one. Here in Seattle, it seems like everyone has a talent.

On one street corner, a magician rips a hundred-dollar

bill into a million little pieces. And then poof! It's back together again. In the park, a pack of shirtless guys are doing the coolest break-dance moves I've ever seen, twisting themselves into pretzels, spinning on their heads, doing endless backflips over one another. There are these people dressed as statues who don't move an inch no matter what you do or say. I know because Charlie and I tried to get the guy dressed up as a silver-toned Michael Jackson to laugh and he didn't even crack a smile. So we took a picture with him instead and left a few dollars as a thank-you tip.

And then there are the singers. So many singers, with such beautiful voices. I'd have a heap of competition if I lived here, so I guess I should be glad I don't. Too bad my mind keeps chanting: *LET'S MOVE HERE! TAKE OUT YOUR GUITAR AND JOIN IN! ADD HARMONIES AND SOME FINGER PICKING!* I feel like I've found an instant community, people to collaborate with and harmonize with and talk music and songwriting with until the break of dawn. It's all just waiting here for me.

Charlie and I stop to admire the Olympic sculptures in Pioneer Square. Watch the fishermen hauling buckets of huge skate, perch, and salmon at Pike Place Market. We slide into an old-timey photo booth tucked into a corner and get cozy inside. The machine flashes four times: We smile, make goofy faces, hold up bunny ears behind each other's heads, and throw our arms around each other and kiss. When the strip finally comes out of the machine a few long minutes later, it's well worth the wait. I grab it and claim it as my own.

"I'm going to treasure this forever," I tell Charlie. I'm not kidding.

He takes my hand and leads me down another busy road and through a deserted alley. We stop in front of a rickety building with an old-fashioned marquee above the door. There are no letters on it, no announcement of a movie or show or whatever. I don't get it.

Charlie looks at me with a huge grin on his face.

"What is this place?"

"Your surprise," he tells me.

Charlie hands two tickets and a bunch of cash to the bouncer. Even though the sign on the door clearly states anyone entering needs to be twenty-one, the big burly guy doesn't bother asking us for IDs. Which is a good thing because my real one says I am eighteen, and I left it on the kitchen counter at home anyhow.

"I thought Seattle was my surprise?"

He shakes his head and grins harder as we walk inside.

Charlie hands my guitar case and jacket to the girl at the coat check. Another bouncer opens a door to let us into another room.

Inside, music pounds. Lights explode. The place is packed from the makeshift stage—where one of my most favorite indie bands in the entire world is already playing—to the back of what appears to be a former warehouse space. A sweaty, happy crowd throbs to the beat.

"It's a secret show!" Charlie yells into my ear. "I found out on Snap yesterday and grabbed tickets for us. I know you said you love this band!"

"I do!"

"Your first live show!"

"OhmyGod, it's so cool!" Though the huge drafty room is nondescript, the people and vibe are anything but. I've never seen so many colors of hair, so many tattoos, so many piercings in so many places IRL. It's like the pages of the music magazines I pore over in my room suddenly came to life. I've found my people. My tribe of fellow creatives. Who knew they were so close all along?

I whirl around, stunned that things like this actually happen in the world. There's so much I've been missing locked away in my room, in my little town, in my little existence. There is so much more out here for me, and it's so much more vibrant and exciting than the elaborate re-creations of real life my dad so lovingly built for me when I was growing up, like the savannah in the basement and the beach he set up in the attic, complete with a hot tub, pool toys, and life-size photos of seagulls and dolphins and sharks and whales. I make a vow to myself here and now: *I'm going to grab every last little bit of everything this world has to offer. I will not be a prisoner of my disease a day longer.*

I realize that not only do I need to have a talk with Charlie, but that a long one with my father is way overdue, too. I know now that I can do way more things than I thought possible before tonight. Maybe even a real, non-online college. Somehow. Where there's a will, there's a way. And I have a will of steel.

While I'm thinking big thoughts and taking in the sights and sounds of this amazing place, Charlie weaves his way through the crowd, with me hanging on to his hand and trailing behind. He writhes through people like a sneaky serpent, finding little pockets of space we can fill undetected. Before long, we're right in front of the stage. Bonus points because no one even got mad at us for budging basically an entire concert's worth of people to get there.

I turn to Charlie, beaming. He grabs my hips and we start dancing a way cooler version of the middle school grind. There is so much action going on, so much to watch, but all I see now is Charlie. No one and nothing else in the world matters at the moment.

The band kicks into a real rocker, and the whole place starts jumping, one pulse uniting the diverse crowd. Charlie and I start jumping around like maniacs, too. I'm lost in the electricity of the music and the energy of this place. I've never felt so alive before, and it hits me that I might never get to experience anything like this again. I try to commit every last detail to memory. Every last second.

• • •

Long before I want it to, the music ends. We grab my coat and guitar, and head back out to the piers. I am still so buzzed from the show, it feels like I'm walking on water instead of sidewalk.

"That was amazing!" I yell, probably a little too loudly. It's hard to tell what level my volume knob is at right now—my ears are still ringing from the concert.

"I know," Charlie says, grinning widely.

I throw my head back and whoop even louder. "Live music is the BEST!"

Charlie laughs. "I know!" he yells back at me.

I stop and take his hand. How can I express how he's changed everything for me, from the fact that I never believed a guy could like me because of my disease to what I now believe my future could hold for me? I fumble around in my mind, trying to find the right words. Finally, I settle for a simple "Thank you."

Charlie gives me this adorable curious puppy look, all floppy hair and playful eyes. It's like he knows what I'm thinking even though he can't possibly. "You're welcome," he says. "Now for your turn."

He gently places my guitar case on the ground and unlocks those finicky latches. Then he positions it perfectly to catch coins and hands me my guitar. I step back, holding up my hands in front of me.

"What? No. No way."

"You owe me a song," Charlie tells me.

I'm shaking my head. "I can't do that...here." This isn't tiny Purdue, Washington, this is big-city Seattle. I'm not prepared to debut one of my songs here. Not tonight. Not yet.

"Yes, you can!" Charlie encourages me. "Live shows are the best! You said so yourself!"

"Are you hungry?" I say, patting my stomach. "I'm

hungry, and you're always hungry and remember all those awesome cafés we saw back there?"

"Katie," Charlie says. He sounds so serious, so sincere, I stop talking. "We can either be in a new city under the stars and you *don't* play me a song, or we can keep making this the best night of our lives."

He shrugs. He's so freaking cute. I feel my resolve melting. What he's given me is so much more than a three-minute song. Singing one for him hardly makes a dent in what I owe him after tonight.

"It's up to you," he tells me. "Don't worry about anything else. This isn't about what I or anyone else wants. It's about what you want right now."

What I want to do is make this incredible guy happy. So I give in. I reach for my guitar and sling the strap over my shoulder. Charlie's entire face lights up.

I give the strings a few good strums. When I look up from my guitar, Charlie's got his phone pointed right at me. He's ready to record this moment so it's captured forever. I get instantly self-conscious and my nerves kick in.

"Charlie, don't—"

He smirks and gestures to the nonexistent crowd behind him. It's basically one weird hairy dude who stopped to tie his shoe. "We're waiting!"

I see that he's right; there's nothing to lose here. Not even my dignity. It's just Charlie and me. There's nothing we can't do together.

So I start strumming some chords, softly at first. I'm still feeling a little unsure of myself. But then it's like muscle memory takes over, and I forget that Charlie's recording me. I'm imagining what it would have been like to be onstage tonight instead of in the crowd staring up in awe at the band. The nervous embarrassment exits my body, and in its place comes a supreme confidence in my abilities.

I close my eyes and sing my latest creation, the one I played for Morgan the other night. Once she finally got over telling me about Garver and paid attention, she really liked it and thought it was the best one yet. I hope she's not mad at me anymore. I really need to tell her I'm sorry when I get home. I sing my heart out—for Charlie, for Morgan, for my dad, but most of all for me.

When I open my eyes again, I see Charlie grinning from behind his phone. He's like my good luck charm. The only thing I'll ever need to succeed.

I strum the last chord and realize Charlie's not the only person who liked my song. There's a whole crowd of people I didn't even realize were there, clapping and cheering wildly for me. And while my fans nowhere near amount to the people in the warehouse at the secret pop-up concert tonight, I get a good taste of what it's like to have my music appreciated by more than just my dad, Fred, and Morgan.

I like it. I love it. In fact, I'm pretty sure I'm going to crave a lot more of this in the future.

Charlie throws his arm around a guy who is still clapping after almost everyone else has stopped.

"YEAH! Come on! Give it up for Katie! WOOOOO-OOO!"

He shakes the guy's shoulders like their team has just won the World Series. The guy gives Charlie a weird look, drops a few bucks into my guitar case, and walks off.

Charlie smiles at me. And I can't stop smiling back.

# 17

The train ride back is uneventful but fully awe-some. Which is to say we make out the entire time. No one else is in the car, no one is watching us, and we take full advantage of our solitude.

When we get back to Purdue—which seems even tinier now that I've experienced Seattle—I'm just not ready for the night to end. I text my dad like I promised.

**Back in Purdue. Home soon.**

**Good night?** he texts back.

The absolute best.

**Stay out as long as you want, Peanut. It's true, you're not a child anymore. I trust you to stay safe and take care of yourself. Charlie is a lucky guy.**

**Thanks,** I text back, happy tears filling my eyes. **You have no idea how much that means to me.**

We get in Charlie's truck and start to drive. I put my phone on do not disturb and sign out of Find My iPhone, asserting my newfound independence and reveling in my dad's hard-earned trust.

Tonight helped me see exactly what I want out of life: my independence. To make my own decisions, my own mistakes, my own way in this big awesome world. I got this.

Charlie and I drive to the beach. We park, then walk slowly down the shoreline. We're in no hurry to get anywhere.

"You were incredible tonight," he tells me.

I make a face like *Come on now.* He's basically starting to rival my dad as my number one fan. It's very sweet, but also kind of mortifying.

"Seriously," he continues, undeterred. "I probably would've said you were good no matter what, but you're *really good.* You have to do something with your songs!"

I've been thinking the same thing all night. A great plan is beginning to form in my head, and it includes my moving to a city; going to college, whether it's only for night classes or researching all the tricks other people with XP use to live a seminormal daytime life; and being a regular, normal student like everyone else. Playing every street corner and open mic night I can find, hoping to be "discovered," but if not, simply taking every opportunity to feel as incredible as I did when I was performing an hour ago.

Music is in my DNA, along with the markers for XP, and I want to share my songs with the world. After tonight, I'm pretty sure that's what I was put on this earth to do. That it's my mission in life. That's how I'll prove I was here even after I'm gone.

And the best part of the future I'm imagining is this: Charlie is in it. I hope he'll be swimming at Berkeley. Is it so crazy to think I could go to school there, too? I've got the grades and the test scores, and they've got the incredible academic programs and performing arts opportunities. I'm sure something could be worked out to accommodate my special needs. It's the perfect plan.

I stop walking. "Are you ready?"

"For what?" he asks.

"To go swimming."

Charlie blinks, surprised. "What? No. I don't swim anymore."

"Yes, you do," I tell him. "You just haven't swum in a while. And I've never been in this water before, so you're gonna take me."

Charlie shakes his head. "Seriously, I don't want to."

I stick my hands on my hips. He is not getting off this easy. He can't ruin our perfect future together by not cooperating. "I didn't want to sing! You made me!"

"That was different," he says, staring down at the sand.

"No, it was not!" I stomp my foot for emphasis.

Charlie laughs. "Easy there, kiddo. Do you have any idea how cold that water is?"

I stare out into the dark ocean, then back at Charlie. I actually have zero clue, other than the hint I've just been given. But it's too late to back down now; too much rides on what happens next.

"Charlie. We can either have come all the way to the beach under the stars and we *don't* go swimming, or we can jump into this water and keep having the best night of our lives. What do you want to do? *Right now?*"

Sure, I stole his own speech and turned it around on him. Whatever it takes. As they say, all's fair in love and war.

Charlie gives me a smirk like he thinks he's won this particular battle. "I don't have a bathing suit."

I smirk right back at him. "Neither do I."

I pull my T-shirt over my head. And then I'm standing in front of him in my bra and jeans. His eyes go wide, but he doesn't move. He's calling my bluff.

I toss my sneakers in the sand and shimmy out of my pants. It's too late to back out now. I'll keep peeling off layers until he agrees.

"Are you coming?" I ask, running toward the water in my underwear.

I turn around as the first wave laps my toes. They basically go numb. I'm not sure how I'm going to make myself dive all the way in; all I know is that it's going to happen. Charlie already has his shirt off and he's struggling to get out of his shorts. I laugh at his sudden enthusiasm.

I turn back toward the water, take a deep breath, and go charging in.

"OH MY GOD! It's freezing!" I whoop.

Charlie throws his head back. "I know!" he yells, and runs in after me.

Our happiness echoes off the ocean. I feel like it knows we're meant to be together.

"Do you like to swim?" Charlie asks me.

I shrug. "I guess. I mean, I don't have all that much experience."

His mouth falls open like he can't believe I'm so deprived. "We have to change that. When are we ever going to be in another situation where I genuinely have moves? Here. Let me show you some."

My heart quickens in the darkness. "You're going to show me your moves?"

"Yep," he says, grabbing me and basically laying me down in the water. And then he's holding me there, his touch gentle but firm.

I can't believe I never knew how great it is to feel so close to someone both physically and mentally. Sometimes, when Charlie and I are lying next to each other kissing, it's like I want to melt right into him.

Before I met Charlie, I had given up on ever falling in love in real life, and with that, ever having sex with anyone. It hasn't happened yet, but the truth is, I wouldn't say no if the opportunity presented itself someday in the not-so-distant future.

"Okay, this one's called freestyle," he says, showing me how to reach out and draw my arm back to move forward. "It's, like, the most basic stroke of them all."

I give it a go but end up flailing around instead of

gliding through the water like Charlie did. "Like this?" I ask him.

He laughs. "That is what we call the doggie paddle."

"Fine, then," I say. "Show me another one."

He launches into another demonstration. "Okay, for this one you push your palms backward along your hips at the end of the pull. That's the butterfly."

All I know is that Charlie's running his hands down the sides of my body is making me want to get out of the water, start a fire, wrap up in a blanket with him, and make "someday" today. But I haven't accomplished my goal yet, so I force myself to concentrate on the task at hand.

"That one's too hard! Next!"

"Next is the breast stroke," Charlie tells me.

"Is this a trick?"

"No," he says, gathering me close to him. "Okay, maybe."

I wrap my arms around his neck and smile up at him. "See? This isn't so bad. You don't actually hate the water."

He gives me the best look ever, like he's drowning in my eyes. "I don't hate anything when I'm with you."

I stare back at him. I believe in him and everything he says. The stars wink down at us, like they're blessing our union.

His lips find mine and we kiss like we've spent our whole lives starving for each other. I cannot get enough of Charlie Reed and I absolutely know the feeling is mutual. The heat gets hotter. It's like we can't possibly get close enough, but then we do.

# 18

Charlie and I are lying together wrapped in a plush blanket he keeps in the back of his truck. I check my watch. It's late—far past my curfew—but there's still time. Sunrise isn't for another few hours. I'm grateful my dad finally gave me the freedom to decide when the night is over.

"You need to get home?" Charlie asks.

"Soon…but not yet." I wish my answer could be *not ever*. Charlie pulls me closer and we snuggle into each other.

"Have you thought any more about Berkeley?" I whisper.

He stares up at the stars. "I keep thinking about after the surgery, when I couldn't swim, and I just...didn't know who I was. At all. And neither did anyone else. I've been in school with these people for years, and they just see me as the guy in the pool. Then when I wasn't in the pool anymore, it was like I was no one to them. And I just think that's bullshit. I'm not worthless if I'm not a swimmer. I don't have to live that life. Just because I liked doing something for a long time doesn't mean I can't change my mind."

I nod. "I get that," I say, and I truly do.

But I can't help feeling there's something more underneath what he just told me. Maybe it's a fear of failure or pride he can't get past. I don't want him wasting a chance to expand his horizons on useless emotions like that.

"But I also know what it feels like to watch people living life from the sidelines," I continue. "You don't want that either. You might not want to be just the guy in the pool, but you're not the guy who doesn't try either. Maybe you won't end up on the team, but don't you want to see if you could? I would."

Something profound and true hits me. I realize this

is how I have to live my life from here on out. I think it applies equally well to Charlie.

"Do everything you can right now and then decide. Because now is all that matters," I tell him.

Charlie kisses my shoulder. He looks like he's deep in thought. "Maybe I'll call the coach tomorrow," he says. "And speaking of tomorrow, I hope you're ready for the greatest sunrise on the planet."

I gasp as the adrenaline kicks in. I look up at the sky. Blackness is giving way to a light purple. I check my watch again: 1:42.

There's a brief moment of relief before I realize something is really wrong. The second hand on my watch isn't moving.

"What time is it, Charlie?" I whisper, horrified.

"Four fifty."

I feel the life drain out of me. "It's not waterproof," I say, almost to myself.

"What isn't?" Charlie asks.

I jump up, frantically grabbing my clothes and cell phone. I click off the do not disturb icon and see I have fourteen missed calls from my dad. How could I have thought I didn't need him watching over me anymore, even for a second?

"Oh my God!"

How can I undo what I did? I'm such an idiot. Dad never should have trusted me. Tears stream down my face as I start sprinting back up toward the road. Maybe I can still race the dark to my house. I'm young. I'm fast.

I hear Charlie's footsteps crashing behind me. "Just stay until the sun—"

"I have to go!" I yell back at him over my shoulder. "Please, we have to leave now! PLEASE!"

"What's wrong?"

But I'm sobbing too hard and time is too precious to answer.

"Katie! Tell me!"

I keep running and running. The sky is turning from a deep violet to a pale blue. I'm never going to make it home before the sun is up, but I still have to try. For me. For my dad. For Morgan. For Charlie, who's never going to forgive himself once he finds out why I'm so panicked even though he did absolutely nothing wrong. Even though *my* bad decisions are what led to all this.

Gravel spews up behind me in the parking lot. Charlie pulls up in his truck and rolls down the window. "Katie, you're scaring me. What the hell is going on?"

I jump into the passenger seat. "Just go!" I scream.

Charlie guns the engine. The truck flies down the road, faster, faster. But no mode of transportation barring time travel could beat the sun now, especially not this old junker. The first hint of sunlight is cresting over the hill behind us. Crepuscular rays—those lines of light little kids always draw around the sun—stream forth from the fiery yellow star. I've never seen anything so beautiful or terrifying in my whole life.

"You have to get me home, Charlie," I beg, even though I know he's doing everything possible. The absolute best he can.

He floors it. The truck lurches ahead. But it's just not going to be enough to save me.

We screech up to my house a few minutes later. I open the door before we've even skidded to a stop. I tumble out of the passenger seat and go sprinting for my house.

The sun is rising above the hills now, rays piercing through the trees in my yard. I feel them, warm on my skin. My arms. My face. I'm fully exposed. I feel warm, then burning hot. I am on fire.

I pound on the door, but my dad doesn't come. I fumble for my key and finally get it into the lock. I throw open the front door and shoot inside. It slams behind me as I fall to the ground, trembling and crying. The only thing

I can do now is pray I haven't caused myself irreparable damage. It's still possible.

Anything's possible, right? Maybe all that will happen is I get a bad sunburn and a big fat lecture from my dad. Miracles happen.

Charlie's pounding on the other side of the door. "Can you just talk to me, Katie?"

But I can't. How could I? What would I say?

Charlie keeps knocking and calling my name.

I run upstairs to get away from it. From him. I've ruined everything. Everything. Nothing can ever be okay again.

From my room, I peer out the window. Charlie still hasn't left. My dad's car squeals up to the curb. He slams the door, looking like he's seen a thousand and one ghosts. Like he's aged a million years in a single night. Morgan is with him. Even though she's mad at me, she's with him.

I'd do anything to take back the pain I've caused everyone. To myself. I've never felt so alone in my life.

"Is she in there?" I can hear my dad screaming. He has Charlie by the shoulders and is shaking him, as if that can rewind time. "Is she inside?"

Dad bursts through the door before Charlie can answer.

Outside, Morgan is still yelling at Charlie. "How could you let this happen?"

"Let *what* happen?" Charlie yells back. He looks like a bewildered little boy, running his hands through his hair until it stands on end every which way.

The sad truth of the situation finally dawns on Morgan. And on me. "She never told you? She swore to us that she did!"

"Told me what?" Charlie looks pale and shaken.

Here it comes. The words that will change everything. The words I should've said to him myself.

"She's sick, Charlie. Katie's sick," Morgan tells him.

"What are you talking about?"

"She has a disease. XP. She can't be in the sun at all," Morgan explains. "It could kill her."

She runs inside after my dad, leaving Charlie standing all alone. On the outside looking in. Trying to digest the worst news possible.

I'm not who he thought I was. Not by a long shot.

# 19

"I'm so, so sorry." I'm saying it to Morgan, but it's for my dad, too. It's the first thing I've said since they found me in my room. I was silent when they asked me if I was okay, I was silent as they handed me clothes for going outside, I was silent the whole car ride over.

Because what could I say?

After so many years of being responsible and safe, after finally convincing my dad I could take care of myself, it turns out I couldn't.

I lied to my dad and Morgan. I lied to Charlie. But my silence also came from the crushing realization that I'd been lying to myself, too.

"It's okay," Morgan says. I guess having a near-death experience makes people forgive you really fast.

"No, Morgan, I'm really sorry." She grabs my hand and I know that she understands that I mean I'm not just sorry for making her worry but that I'm also sorry for everything I said to her.

"We love you more than anything, Peanut," my dad tells me.

It makes me feel even worse that they're not mad at me. That they're just worried and sad and spent. It's all my fault.

The three of us are sitting in stiff plastic chairs in the hospital waiting room where Dr. Fleming has an office. I'm completely exhausted, though I'm not sure at this point whether it's more emotional or physical.

My face is burning up. My arms feel like they're engulfed in flames. Morgan assures me this is how normal people feel after a few too many hours in the sun. But I'm not so sure. It feels ominous.

Even more ominous is my dad's face right now. He's grinding his teeth. His eyebrows are furrowed so tightly together that they fuse into a single entity. He sits with his head in his hands, like it's too heavy for his neck to hold up anymore.

"Why do they use such uncomfortable chairs?" Morgan muses. "We're here to get healthy, and we're gonna leave with back issues."

My dad tries to smile at her. It comes off more like a grimace. I give her a little chuckle that turns into a sob.

"I'm sure everything's fine," Morgan says, putting a hand on my leg. "It was just for a second, if that. This is nothing. We're all good here."

Except that while she's assuring me nothing's wrong, we're both staring at the girl in the waiting room who's about my age. Her hands and head shake; her skin is covered in lesions and dark sores. We all know that might be me next.

My favorite nurse appears. "We're ready for you, Katie."

Dad goes to stand, but I put a hand out to stop him. "I'll go myself this time." If I'm old enough to practically kill myself by being so irresponsible, then I'm also old enough to face the consequences of my actions.

Dad nods. As I follow the nurse into the office area, Garver bursts through the hospital doors. He runs over to Morgan. She falls into his arms crying.

"Is she okay?" Garver asks.

Morgan doesn't answer. She just buries her head in his shoulder and falls apart. I must look like the walking dead for her to be so upset. I wonder if I actually am.

Dr. Fleming gives me a warm hug when I get to the exam room. "It's been a while, Katie," she says, pulling back to take a closer look at me. "You've grown into a beautiful young woman."

"I'm sorry I haven't been at my appointments lately," I tell her, climbing up onto the examining table with heavy, wooden legs.

Dr. Fleming offers an understanding smile. "Sometimes I think XP is harder on parents than patients. He was just trying to protect you."

"And look how I thanked him for all his sacrifices." I want to cry, but it's like I have no tears left in me at this point.

"There's no sense in looking backward, Katie," Dr. Fleming tells me. "And we'll deal with whatever is in front of us together. Okay?"

I nod. Nurse Jane takes vial after vial of blood while I stare at the brightly colored murals painted on the wall. I've learned over the years that it hurts less if I can't see the needle or all that deep red liquid coming out of me. Some vampire I am, huh?

Next, I'm wheeled into the CAT scan room. I want to protest that I can walk there, but to be honest, I'm grateful not to have to. I lie there as still as possible as the lights and sounds of the machine whir around me. I guess I fall asleep, because the next thing I know it's over and Nurse Jane is telling me it's time to go back to the exam room.

There, Dr. Fleming and Jane put on these huge magnifying goggles that look like virtual-reality headsets. They proceed to carefully examine every inch of my body, talking in cryptic code the whole time.

"Dysplastic nevus, four millimeters."

"Congenital nevus, growth noted."

"Grouping of new lentigines here."

And so on and so on. I wait and listen, wondering what it all means. Wondering what Charlie is thinking right now. If he hates me for lying to him. If I'll ever see him again.

And how can I? Dad will never let that happen. Besides, why would Charlie want to see me after the way I betrayed his trust?

It's over, I conclude. I was lucky to have him while I did. To experience something I never thought I would. Time to go back to being Rapunzel stuck in my room forever. I was a fool to think I could ever go to college and have a long-term relationship like a normal person.

Finally, Dr. Fleming says to me, "Okay, you can sit up now, Katie. I'll go get your father while you get dressed. Meet me back in my office as soon as you're ready."

I pull on my leggings, drag my sweatshirt back over my head, and stuff my feet into my Converse. I trudge down the long hall and sit in the chair in front of Dr. Fleming's impressively large mahogany desk. My dad is already seated in the chair next to me, staring straight ahead.

"The sunlight exposure was minimal," Dr. Fleming begins. "The physical effects you're seeing right now will heal."

My dad puts his hand on my arm and we smile at each other. Maybe I didn't ruin everything after all.

"But—"

Dad winces.

My stomach drops.

"As you know, your specific kind of XP generally lies dormant until a triggering event," she continues. "We won't know if that's what this was until we get the results from your blood work and CT scans."

My dad leans forward in his chair. "And if this was? A triggering event?"

I hold my breath, waiting for Dr. Fleming's answer.

"We'll cross that bridge if we come to it," she says. "If you notice any symptoms, Katie—unexpected shaking, muscle pain, loss of motor function—you have to promise to tell me immediately."

I nod. My hands are shaking as we speak. Is that a symptom, or just me being tired and scared? Everything feels like a sign right now.

"Any word on the UW study?" my dad asks as we get up to leave.

"I followed up with them last week," Dr. Fleming says. "No news yet."

I hope in this case that no news is good news. My dad deserves less bad news in his life.

●  ●  ●

I completely crash when I get home, falling into one of those heavy, dreamless sleeps that feel like I'm lost in a big black void. I wake up much later, groggy and crabby. I don't want to eat or watch a movie or even talk to anyone.

Morgan comes over and knows me well enough to just be with me, together but doing our own thing. I strum my guitar mindlessly, the chords coming out sounding dissonant and out of key. Morgan pretends to read Dear Gabby, but she doesn't ever scroll to a new question.

My phone vibrates constantly. I ignore it. Nothing good can come of answering Charlie's texts. Better to cut communication off completely and move on than drag this thing out when the end result will be the same no matter what.

"I know I told you to play hard to get, but you have to at least see what he has to say," Morgan tells me.

I shake my head even as my phone vibrates again. Morgan tosses aside her phone, grabs mine, and starts reading the texts.

"He's asking you if he can come over to talk to you—"

"Don't," I tell her. "Just delete them."

"Katie…"

I look up, my eyes locking onto Morgan's. "If I read them, I'll write back, and then he'll write back, and then we'll meet up, which we can't. No."

"Why can't you? You don't need to be a martyr to protect Charlie's delicate feelings. He's a big boy, I'm sure he can handle—"

I stop her midsentence. For the first time ever, Morgan has no idea how I'm feeling. "*I* can't handle it, okay?"

I yell, tears streaming down my face. "I can't. He's just gonna get hurt. And I can't be the one who hurts him. Now will you please just delete them?"

I can tell Morgan doesn't want to. I know she hates how much I'm hurting right now. That she's even willing to forgive me for being an awful cranky beast and yelling at her when none of this is her fault.

"Okay," she says quietly, clicking through my phone. Deleting, deleting, deleting.

I nod gratefully and go back to my guitar. But it's just not sounding right tonight. Morgan watches me for a second, then picks her phone back up. I strum and realize my fingers are on the wrong strings, the wrong frets.

I hold up my hand. My fingers are shaking uncontrollably. I push my guitar away before Morgan can notice.

But I know.

I *know*.

# 20

I can't sleep even though I'm tired. I can't eat even though I'm hungry. I toss and turn, throw the blankets on and off because I'm alternately shivering and then sweating. I hear a car door slam, then the doorbell ring.

I get out of bed and look out the window. It's Dr. Fleming. In all the years I've been seeing her, she's never come here—I always go to see her at the hospital. She's far too busy to make house calls.

This is not a good sign. Although she's not delivering any news I don't already assume.

My dad steps out onto the porch and closes the front door behind him. I can't hear what Dr. Fleming says to him, but the next thing I know, he's yelling, "We should do another set of tests. They could come back different!"

"Her brain has begun to contract," Dr. Fleming says, loudly enough for me to hear this time. "Once the neural pathways start—"

"What about the study?" my dad bellows. "What about UW? There has to be—"

"They shut it down," Dr. Fleming tells him, putting a hand on his shoulder. "I found out this morning. There won't be a phase two."

My dad breaks down at this news. He's always been so strong. He's never cried in front of me, not even when my mom died. And now he's a wreck because of me. Because of my actions.

"I did everything I was supposed to," he says, choking out the words. "When she was little, no matter how much she cried and moaned, I wouldn't let her go outside. Play in the park. Go to the beach. She *begged* me. For things she had every right to do, and I denied her all of them. To protect her. And for what? For *this*?"

Dr. Fleming pats my father's back as emotion overcomes him. "XP is a disease that tends to take the joy out of a child's life," she tells him. "But all these years I've known Katie, she's never complained, never sulked, only seen the good in things. And the way she talks about you—I've never seen a teenager so openly adore her father."

She's crying along with Dad now. And I'm crying with them both. They hug.

"Katie's not only held on to her joy, she brings other people joy. Katie shines brighter than almost any patient I've ever treated. And that's because she's so well loved. You're a good father, Jack."

My dad swipes at his face with his sleeve and nods. "How long?"

"It's hard to know for sure," Dr. Fleming tells him.

"Days? Weeks? Months? What?"

And in typical Dr. Fleming fashion, she tells him, "Most likely one of those."

I feel numb, like I'm frozen in time. I can't do anything but blame myself for ruining everyone's life, including my own. How could I have been so ungrateful? This is what I get for not wanting the life I had anymore, for wanting so much more. I get to have no life at all. A life cut even shorter than it already was going to be.

I've got to make this better somehow.

• • •

I'm sitting with my dad in the darkroom later. He's dipping photos in solution, drying them, hanging them. Doing what he does best.

"You know I know, right?"

He stops what he's doing. Stares at me. Clears his throat. "What?"

"I heard you and Dr. Fleming talking on the porch earlier. When you thought I was sleeping," I tell him.

Dad comes over and scoops me up in a hug. "I'm sorry," he says over and over. "I'm so sorry."

I tell him *It's okay* and *I'm sorry, too* more times than I can count. I've been thinking all day about how I can possibly make some meaning out of this awful situation, and what I've finally come up with is this: I have to find a way to give back. One last message of love. I suddenly know what I can do for my dad.

"I'll be upstairs," I tell him. "When you're done down here, we can order some takeout, okay?"

"That's it, Katie?" he asks, palms up, with a little shrug. "No questions?"

I shake my head. "Nope."

An hour later, he makes his way to the den. I'm sitting on the couch still typing away on my computer. I've been working hard on my masterpiece, and it's almost complete.

"I'm starving," my dad says. "Should we order from Hunan Chinese?"

I make one last change and look up at him. "Huh?"

"I said, are you in the mood for Chinese?" he says. "What are you so engrossed in?"

I turn my computer around so he can see it. "Chinese, sure, always. You know that. And I've been making you an online dating profile."

My dad is momentarily floored. "*What?*" he asks, his mouth hanging open.

But really now. This is a long time coming. No one should have to be alone. Everyone should have someone special. That's basically the key to happiness, as I found out with Charlie.

"What do you think?" I ask, showing him two different

options for his profile picture. "I like your hair in this one, but in the other you have your camera."

Dad tries to force my laptop shut. "Nope. This is not happening—"

I stay firm. "This—is—happening! You need to go on some dates! You can even help me write it. Sit."

My dad starts to protest again, but I shoot him my most serious look. He seems to accept that I'm not joking around here and will not give up on this idea. He plops down next to me.

"Here's what I have so far. *World's greatest father and handsomest photographer—*"

My dad makes a buzzer noise. "Veto."

I ignore him and continue. *"Looking for fellow adventurer interested in art, photography, nostalgia about the SuperSonics—"*

"SuperSonics, now that's important," my dad says, nodding.

*"And a partner in crime to travel the world."* I look up to see whether he is getting all this.

But he's staring off into space, at the wall, at one of the pictures he and my mom took way back when. "I don't travel," he finally says, shaking his head.

"You will, though," I tell him. I don't add the second

part of what I'm thinking, which is: *You can again. After I'm gone.*

It's like my dad hears my unspoken thoughts. The air is basically sucked out of the room. He gets up off the couch and turns to leave. "All right, we're not talking about this—"

I grab his sleeve. "Please. I want to. I *have* to."

He stops. Exhales long and loudly, like a creaky old radiator. I pat the couch next to me.

"We had each other before. And now…" I am trying to gather my courage to say what neither of us has acknowledged out loud yet. "We lost Mom, and you're gonna lose me, too."

"No!" my dad protests. "There's always a chance that—"

"I know it sucks. For you probably even more than me. But reality is reality," I tell him. "We've always known it's a matter of when, not *if*… and it is going to happen, like it or not."

Nothing in history has ever been so hard to say. From the looks of my dad, nothing in history has ever been so hard to hear. But we need to talk about these things while we still can. He needs to know how much I love and appreciate everything he's done for me.

I take a deep breath and continue my speech. "I want

you to travel and start photographing the world again. I want everyone to see your photos, Dad."

And with that, he breaks down in tears. In front of me. Another first. I'm honestly kind of proud of him. For so many years we've pretended to be okay to each other. And now it's okay to let each other know we're not.

I want my dad to know that some good can come of this—that he can have all his dreams back when I'm gone if he'll only let himself. That I want more than anything for him to be whole again. And that he can be, even without me or Mom. He has to be or I won't be able to bear what comes next.

"Stop," my dad says through his tears. "I can't…"

I forge ahead even though it's hard to weather his grief. "I just want you to have as great a life as the one you've given me. I need to know you'll try to be happy, and have adventures and someone to share them with because… well, that's the best part."

Dad composes himself with a few deep cleansing breaths, like we learned from those meditation videos we tried a while back. When I can see he's almost ready to agree, I try to close the deal fast.

"Just go on one date," I urge him. "Pick a rando lady and take her out. *Please*."

He finally nods. "Okay."

I grab his hand in mine. "Promise."

"I promise," he tells me.

I wrap my arms around him and we hug each other tightly. My tears fall fast on his shoulder. His tears soak into mine. I'm the first to break away.

"Now let's call Hunan Chinese," I say, wiping my face on my shoulder.

Dad gives me a smile, and says, "You go upstairs and rest for a bit. I'll order us dinner."

My heart feels like it's somehow stitching itself back together. I know I can still make a difference for as long as I'm here. And maybe even after if I work fast enough.

# 21

The doorbell rings forty-five minutes later, so I head downstairs.

"Our dinner is served," I yell as I take the last step and see my dad still sitting on the couch.

"Hey, can you get that, honey?" he asks, his eyes never leaving the baseball game on the TV screen. "It's full count with two outs and two men on base."

I laugh at how intense he's being about a regular-season matchup. "Sure."

I walk to the door and open it. My mouth falls open. It's not our delivery guy after all.

I slam the door shut and fall against it. "I think you better come here!" I yell to my dad.

But he's already standing right in front of me. "I think you better let him in," he says, offering me a hand up. I take it.

"How did you know it was Charlie?"

"Because I'm the one who called him," he says. "Having someone to share your life with is the best part, right? Isn't that what you just told me?"

"I can't see him," I whisper. "I mean . . . can I?"

"Go," he says, opening the door and shooing me outside. "Talk."

Charlie's standing there, holding out two bags from Hunan Chinese. After a moment, he says, "Dinner is served?" and we both laugh a little. How does he do that? Take an awkward moment and make it feel . . . not as awkward. Still, his ease doesn't make me feel any less uneasy. It's like the first time we met all over again.

"You do exist," he says. "This time I was positive I dreamed you."

I start to smile but stop when I realize that this is not what I came out here to do. I know what my dad said and

I know what I want. But if there's one thing I'm sure of, it's that you can't always get what you want in this life. This is for closure. My gift to Charlie so he can move on: letting him go.

"I'm sorry I didn't tell you, that was unforgivable, and I wish I could make it up to you, but unfortunately, this arrangement"—I gesture to him and then me, indicating, y'know, us—"it, it…can't go on." My speech is coming out oddly formal and stilted. I take a deep breath and try to sound normal. "You and I continuing to see each other is just…a really bad idea, and I—"

Ugh. I look up at Charlie and he's biting his bottom lip. He looks like he's going to laugh, not cry, like I was worried he might. Now I feel dumber than ever. I start over.

"Look, love is never fair, but this is particularly unfair, like *Guinness Book of Records* unfair, and so it should stop. It's done. It's not you; it's me."

I wince. That was even more awkward.

"Good-bye," I say in closing, holding my hand out to shake his. He just stares at it. When he looks back up at me, his face is lit with one of the biggest smiles I've ever seen.

"That was, like, the worst breakup speech I've ever heard," he tells me.

I don't get it. He's not accepting my breakup? That's not even a thing as far as I know. "What?"

Charlie rolls his eyes at me. "A D minus would be generous. Zeroes from all the judges. A total flop."

"I've never done this before!" I protest before realizing what's underneath what he's saying: He doesn't want us to break up, even after everything that's happened. And everything that's inevitably going to happen. "But seriously, we can't."

"We can, though," he tells me.

I stop talking and gaze into those melty eyes of his. My resolve melts with them. I want to believe we can. But how?

He shrugs like he actually heard my unspoken question. "We can," he repeats. "What I *can't* do is stop seeing you. I tried it and it sucks. And"—here he makes his fingers into quotation marks and his voice sound formal like I did before—"it can't go on."

I laugh, but the pain I feel is very real. I don't want to hurt him more than I already have. That would kill me before the stupid XP does. "Charlie..."

He jumps back in before I can start protesting again. "Katie. You can either have spent the past few weeks changing my life and becoming my favorite person only to leave me standing on your lawn like a chump, or we can keep making this the best summer of our lives."

I shake my head. He's crazy. Most guys would be running for the hills and thanking their lucky stars I let them off the hook so easily. And here Charlie is, trying to convince me we should stay together even though our relationship is completely doomed.

"I've done my research," Charlie says, dead serious now. "I know what XP is. I know what's going on. But we're not people who don't try. You knew that before I did."

I finally break down, laughing *and* crying. Why choose, when both fit the moment so well?

"I'm not gonna sit back and watch this happen," he tells me. "The choice is mine and I'm making it. I want to be with you."

I wipe my eyes. Look into his. Throw my arms around his neck and kiss him like my life depends on it. And in some ways, maybe it does. It's the kind of kiss—real and passionate—people probably wait their whole lives to experience, and I'm lucky enough to have mine now.

I realize that even in the worst of times there's always a ray of hope. Charlie is mine.

• • •

As I'm sitting on the couch between my dad and Charlie a little later, happily slurping up lo mein, I can't help thinking that despite the enormous poop sandwich I've been dealt I'm still grateful for everything my life has given me. For everything I don't have—my mom, a group of friends, the hope of a happily ever after—there's so much I do have. And always have had. And now there's Charlie. I think about what he said to me earlier, and I feel the exact same way: He exists. I didn't dream him up. And as sure as I feel his warmth next to me on the couch as his leg brushes against mine, I know that we're not just a summer fling. That what we feel for each other is everlasting. That nothing can tear us apart.

Nothing. And that includes dying.

# 22

I have to beg and plead, but I convince my dad to go see Charlie's big return to the pool. He's been working his butt off ever since we swam together on what turned out to be both the best night and worst day of my life. And I'll be damned if I'm not going to be there to cheer him on along with everyone who ever supported him in swimming, including his friends, family, and former coach—and, I hope, a new one from Berkeley.

It's kind of a pain to prepare for the trip to the high

school pool—I have to slather myself in three coats of extra-strength prescription sunscreen and dress in thick layers that don't match the summery weather. Dad has to apply a special protective film to the windows of his car to prevent UV rays from penetrating them, plus install basically what's like a two-way mirror between the front seat and the back. As in he can see behind him but I can't see through it and no light can get through. It's a weird way to travel, like I am someone überfamous in a limo, too snobby to interact with my driver.

"Come on, Dad," I say, trying to jolly him out of the fear I see in his eyes. He has to get over the dread that has kept us from venturing out much for all these years. Especially now, when it really doesn't matter how careful we are anymore. "What's the worst thing that could happen? I could have a triggering event? Too late, I already did."

His lips stay pressed together in a thin line. "Not funny."

"Gallows humor," I tell him with a shrug.

It's so hard to get used to the new realities each day brings. I feel old and sorry for myself, like everything that made me *me* is quickly being stripped away. That before long I'll be nothing but a shell of my former self. The day

I realized I couldn't play guitar anymore was the absolute worst. I cried harder than I have in my life, not only because music has always been my greatest source of pleasure and pride but because it's also been my longstanding hope to leave my songs as my parting gift to this world. And now that can never happen.

Charlie is the only one who can make me forget how fast I'm going downhill. He somehow still makes me feel like the most beautiful, talented, normal, healthy girl in the world. He acts like he doesn't even notice the stuff I can't do anymore.

It's when I'm alone that I find myself on the verge of a constant panic attack. I'm terrified about what might get taken from me next, not to mention what will happen once there's nothing left to take. I don't want to leave this planet. I'm not ready. I probably never will be.

Basically, everything that's happening to me physically since that morning on the beach has been horrifying and terrifying and terrible. The only upside I can see is that at a certain point it at least stopped being surprising. So there's that.

"Sometimes the only way to deal with the really bad stuff is to laugh at it," I tell my dad. "Now let's go watch Charlie get his scholarship to Berkeley back."

"One, two, three, run!" my dad says, grabbing his keys.

I pull the strings of my hoodie as tight as they can go, until only the tiniest bit of my eyes are showing. Dad and I used to play this game to get me to the car for appointments when I was younger. I appreciate the nod to tradition today.

Naturally, the preparations for the ride took much longer than the ride itself. We're at the Purdue High natatorium in less than ten minutes. Dad parks as close as possible to the building, and we make another dash inside.

It's humid and sticky on the pool deck. I immediately start sweating underneath my many layers of clothes. I go to unzip my hoodie.

My dad reaches out a hand to stop me. He points at the wall of windows on the opposite side of the pool. The midday sun is streaming through, splashing rainbow colors onto the puddles of the pool deck. "Don't. It's not safe."

"What's the worst thing—" I start to say again, but then I notice the worry lines on my dad's forehead. They seem to have grown in size and number over the past few weeks. "No problem, Dad."

We climb into the packed stands and take a seat in the corner of the highest bleacher, where the sun can't possibly hit me. I see Charlie's parents sitting in the front row.

Zoe's there, too, along with her crew. She sees me and gives me a fake smile and wave. "Hi, Katie Price!"

"New friend of yours?" my dad asks.

"Old enemy," I reply, waving back and giving Zoe an even faker smile than the one she gave me. So she figured out who I was. I feel surprisingly calm; it's like Zoe has lost all her power over me. The worst has already happened. Nothing she could do to me would ever compare.

Then I spot the reason we're all here: a fit-looking man in a Berkeley polo shirt holding a clipboard, furiously taking notes, a stopwatch around his neck. He looks up and notices me noticing him. I give him a smile and a thumbs-up. His lips curve up almost imperceptibly, but I take it as a good omen anyhow.

"Next up, the last event of the day—the finals of the men's two-hundred-meter freestyle!" the announcer booms. His voice bounces off the tiled walls. Cheers erupt in the stands. The place feels completely electric.

The swimmers file out and take their places next to their respective starting blocks. I silently bemoan the fact that everyone looks the same in their Speedos, swim caps, and goggles. I crane my neck, trying to figure out which guy is Charlie. He texted me earlier that he'd be swimming in lane one, but that can't be right. The block is empty.

Charlie's parents clutch at each other. Dad turns to me and raises his eyebrows. I shrug and shake my head like *I have no idea. He's supposed to be there.* Berkeley man stops writing and glances down at his watch and then back up impatiently.

I hold my breath. And then, like magic, there he is. Charlie looks so powerful, so strong, so goddamn *good*, I want to jump out of the stands and throw my arms around him.

The other swimmers are splashing water on themselves, shaking the nervous energy out of their arms and legs. But Charlie just stands there looking cool, calm, and collected. He grins at his mom and dad.

He keeps searching the stands with his eyes, looking through bleacher after bleacher. My dad finally lifts his hand and points down at me. I push the hoodie off my head—Dad doesn't object this time—and wave. Charlie breaks into a huge smile and pats his heart. I pat mine. It's our new code: *Amor vincit omnia.* Love conquers all.

Charlie nods. He's ready to go now.

"Set," the announcer rumbles.

The swimmers get into position.

*BEEP!*

And they're off. The competitors spend most of the first lap underwater. I'm breathless just watching, so I can't imagine how they must feel.

Suddenly, they all break to the surface. The graceful silence is replaced by water churning beneath determined arms and legs. To me, it seems like all the swimmers are in a tie. It's still anyone's race.

Charlie's parents grip each other's hands. The Berkeley coach looks up at the clock on the scoreboard, then back at the pool. The swimmers head into lap number two.

The guy in the lane next to Charlie starts pulling ahead. Everyone else stays in a tight clump behind him. I stick two fingers into either side of my mouth and whistle as loudly as I can, trying to motivate Charlie to go faster, faster.

The swimmers flip, turn, and rocket into the third lap. The guy in the lead puts even more distance between himself and the rest of the pack. *Come on, Charlie,* I think. *This is your big chance. Give it everything you've got. Your future depends on it.*

One lap to go. Charlie is still behind, in third or maybe even fourth place. I leap to my feet and start screaming, cheering as loudly as I've ever cheered for anything in my life. I hope he can hear me. I know how many hours he's been putting in to get back into shape. I know he's done everything he can to prepare for this moment. I know he can do it.

And then I see it. He's surging. He knows he can do it, too.

Charlie's arms pump harder, harder. He glides through the water. He's coming on strong. Coming up fast. He passes the guy in third place, and then the one in second. But there's still too much space between him and the swimmer in first. Winning now seems close to impossible.

But Charlie just keeps on gaining. And then it happens. His hand touches the wall before anyone else's. He WON!

I keep screaming. That race was probably the most exciting thing I'll ever witness. Totally worthy of getting hoarse over.

Charlie pulls himself out of the pool, shoulders and biceps and abs rippling. Then he takes off his goggles and heads for the stands. I can't help myself; I go running down the bleachers toward him. Toward the light. Dad follows right on my heels.

"Stay clear of the sunny spots, Katie!" he reminds me. I stop short of where Charlie is standing.

The Berkeley coach grabs him for a quick talk, then heads out the door. I start toward Charlie again, but then his parents intercept him. So Dad and I hang back, waiting. Finally, Charlie breaks free from all the well-wishers and scoops me up in a hug.

"You were so good!" I yell.

He puts me back on the ground and beams at me. "I was, wasn't I?"

"You really were! What did the Berkeley guy say?"

"He said he was impressed and would be in touch."

I beam back at him. "In touch is good! I'm so proud of you!"

My dad nudges his way between us, giving Charlie a hearty wallop on the back. "I guess the rumors about you are true," he says. "Congrats, Charlie. You were a maniac in the pool."

"Thank you, Mr. Price," Charlie says. "And thanks for letting Katie come."

My dad looks down at me and smiles. "She wouldn't have missed it for the world."

Charlie's smiling at me, too. "Mr. Price? Would you mind if I borrowed Katie tomorrow night?"

I put my hands together and give Dad a cute look,

like I'm begging him to say yes. He finally nods. "I think that'll be fine, Charlie."

After one last hug, I pull my hoodie tightly over my head again and we make a break for the car. It seems that everyone else did the same, though; the parking lot is jammed. Five minutes later, Dad hasn't even backed out of the space.

I'm staring out the window, exhausted from the outing. I'm so glad I was here to witness Charlie's success. But all I can think about now is getting home and going to bed.

I'm just about to nod off when I see Charlie and his parents leaving the building. He runs up to our car and puts his palm up against the blacked-out backseat window. I put my hand against his from the inside. I'm pretty sure he can sense I'm there.

Mr. Reed taps on the front window and my dad rolls it down. "I just want to tell you and your daughter how much your support has meant to Charlie," he says.

I yell "Same!" from the backseat even though I'm pretty sure he can't hear me.

"He's a wonderful young man," my dad replies.

"And, by all accounts, your Katie is wonderful, too," Mr. Reed says.

I wish I could get out and meet him now, but the sun is shining high overhead at the moment. Too risky even though I've already been exposed.

"I just wanted to tell you how happy I am our kids found each other," Mr. Reed continues. "There are a few people, or moments, in a person's life that change our story. She'll leave her mark on him forever. And him on her. Even though it's not meant to last. As I told Charlie, all you can do is be grateful for the experience, and be grateful she came into your life."

I whip out my phone and text my dad. **Tell him amor vincit omnia!**

My dad pauses, looks down at his phone, then looks back up and laughs. "Katie wants you to know that love conquers all," he tells Mr. Reed.

Mr. Reed laughs along with him. "Well, now, I do believe that's the truth." He taps the back window next to where Charlie and I are virtually "holding hands." "Be well, Katie!"

I pat my heart and press my palm against Charlie's some more. *Amor vincit omnia*, I think. *Love conquers all.*

# 23

Charlie picks me up the next night right on time. I have on another new outfit—ordered online with my dad's blessing. I did my hair and put on makeup carefully, painstakingly. It's getting harder and harder to do even the simplest things lately, but I don't want to miss any chance I might have left to look and feel young and beautiful and alive.

My dad snaps another prom picture of us before we leave, and I don't even protest this time. I don't even feel embarrassed. I just try to feel grateful for the experience, like Mr. Reed said we should. The anxiety that seems to be with me every waking moment lately fades into the background. It's just a little hum instead of a huge shriek.

Charlie holds the door to his truck open for me. I climb in. My dad waves good-bye to us from the front porch.

My hands are trembling in my lap as Charlie hops into the driver's seat. I try to shove them under my legs to hide my shakiness, but he reaches over and takes my hands in his. Then he brings my fingers up to his mouth, kisses them individually, then places my hands back into my lap.

I give him a little smile. He's the only one who could take the awkwardness out of a moment like this. His being so kind doesn't make my situation any easier to accept, but it does make me realize how lucky I am to have him in my life. I settle back into my seat, psyched to find out whatever Charlie has up his sleeve this time.

We pull into the parking lot of a nondescript warehouse-looking place half an hour later. I start smiling and can't stop. "Another pop-up concert?"

"You really think I'm that uncreative?" he says, shaking his head. "Wrong. Come on. You'll see."

"I'll see what?" I ask, following him excitedly.

"You'll see when we get there."

Charlie leads me into what looks like the starship *Enterprise*'s control room. There's a huge mixing console the size of a car with zillions of buttons and levers on it, plus multitrack recorders and digital workstations. Beyond the glass in this room is a studio, complete with musicians getting their instruments ready to perform.

I take it all in. I can't believe I get to see an actual recording happen tonight. It's like a dream come true. "Who are we here to see?"

"Oh, you mean those guys?" Charlie asks, flicking a thumb in their direction. "They're here for you."

A cool bearded dude approaches us before I can even begin to process what Charlie has just said. "You Katie? Let's do this."

"Oh my God, no, no, no—" My eyes get huge and I have the sudden urge to go plan a fake cat funeral. I make a break for the door, but Charlie blocks it.

"Yes, yes, yes, yes."

"How did you? What are...? This is crazy!" I stammer. "How are we paying for this?!"

Charlie shrugs. "Don't worry about it."

This can mean only one thing: He basically just spent his life savings on me. Money he worked so hard for this summer and the summer before that and the summer before that. I know how much a professional recording costs. Way too much. I'm overwhelmed by his generosity. Tears, which are always close to the surface lately, start pooling in my eyes.

"Charlie, no! That's your truck money! You worked so hard for it. I can't let you do this!"

"It's already done," he says, grinning at me. "Besides, most colleges don't let you have a car on campus as a freshman."

"Berkeley called?" I say, reaching out and putting a hand to his cheek.

"Not yet," he says. "But I'm feeling pretty confident they will."

"I'm really, really proud of you," I tell him. "Whether it's at Berkeley or somewhere else—you're going to set this world on fire someday, Charlie Reed."

"And you already are, Katie Price," he tells me. "Now go. Do this. You helped me figure out my dream. It's pay-back time."

He starts pushing me gently toward the studio. I stop him and hold up my hands. They're shaking.

"I can't play anymore," I whisper, my stomach a hot pit of fear and shame.

He takes my hands in his and stares into my eyes. "Just sing. Pretend it's just me."

I nod and try to tap into all the positive vibes he's sending me. He spins me around and pushes me toward the studio. I step through the door into the center of the room. I feel unsure and nervous. I guess I can blame my shaking on that instead of the real reason. Then no one has to feel sorry for the poor dying girl and lie to her about how great her song is if they really don't think so. Maybe I'll finally get some honest feedback from real musicians—people who really know talent.

The guys in the band nod hello as they finish tuning their instruments. The engineer clicks on the speaker from the other room. "Whenever you're ready, Katie, let's lay one down…"

I'm ready now except for one thing. The song choice. I have no clue what I'm supposed to sing. "What are we playing?"

The guitarist, a tattooed, pierced linebacker of a guy, hands me the sheet music everyone in the studio has. I read the title. "Charlie's Song."

"This—this is my song. I've been working on this!" I exclaim, almost to myself. I look up to see Charlie smirking at me through the window of the control room. "How did you get this?"

Charlie clicks the speaker on. "I stole your notebook again."

"You wrote this song?" the guitarist asks.

He looks like he doesn't quite believe me when I nod.

"Not bad," he says with a smile.

I smile back at him and put on my headphones. The drummer counts off a beat and the band starts playing. My song. Charlie's song. It sounds even better than I ever imagined it could.

Music swells around me, and then it's time for me to come in. I step up to the screened mic. I start to sing, softly at first. But with every note, I gain a sense of confidence I didn't even know I had in me.

I close my eyes and sing for everyone I love. I picture my dad developing awesome photos from an exotic trip he takes not too far off in the future. Morgan and Garver still together, even after they head off to different colleges in the fall. Charlie gliding effortlessly through the pool at Berkeley, racking up just as many records there as he did in tiny little Purdue, Washington. And my mom playing her favorite song by Crosby, Stills, Nash & Young.

*"I have walked alone, with the stars in the*
    *moonlit night,*
*I have walked alone, no one by my side.*
*Now I walk with you, with my head held*
    *high,*
*in the darkest night, I feel so alive."*

When the song ends, I know I've nailed it. Charlie is watching from the control room, recording it all with his iPhone. He nudges the engineer, who nods. Do I even see amazement in their eyes? Because I'm amazed at what just came out of me, too.

On the ride home, Charlie and I are both still giddy with excitement. Neither of us wants the night to end, which is how we always feel. Charlie pulls off an unfamiliar exit well before we're back in Purdue.

"Where are we going?" I'm resting my head on his shoulder. Feeling at home. Like somehow everything is right in the world despite everything that's wrong in mine.

"I want to show you somewhere I come to think sometimes," he tells me.

The truck climbs higher and higher until Charlie pulls over and cuts the engine. He gets out of the cab and comes around to my side, opening the door and offering me a hand.

He points at the sky. I look up and gasp. It's like a million stars are staring back at us. Like this overlook is the doorway to heaven itself.

We climb into the back. He's got blankets and pillows and a thermos of hot chocolate waiting there. He pours us each a cup, puts on lids, and hands one to me. I snuggle into his arms.

I take a sip and point up at a star. "Can you name that one?"

"That's Charlinium," he says with a laugh. "Because it's really huge and powerful."

I roll my eyes at him and point to another.

"That one's Burritorium, because it's in the shape of a burrito."

"That's Procyon, silly," I tell him. "Eleven light-years away."

He turns to look at me. "So we were about seven when that light was made?"

I nod. "Good math. That was also when you got your first skateboard, right?"

I watch Charlie's eyes grow wide. "How did you know that?"

I decide I might as well tell him the truth. The whole truth this time. We don't have much time left together.

"Charlie, that night, when we met at the train station...I already knew you."

I can't tell if he's weirded out or creeped out or what. His face is in total neutral, like I just told him it was going to rain tomorrow or something equally benign. "What do you mean?"

I stare up at the sky. "In elementary school, you walked past my window every morning at dawn on your way to swim practice."

I sneak a sideways glance at Charlie. He doesn't look scared, so I keep going. "In third grade, you started skateboarding. In sixth grade, you wore a Ken Griffey Jr. jersey every day for, like, a month. In ninth grade, you buzzed your hair off. I waited for you. It was the best part of my day. So by the time we met, you were already a part of my life."

I finish my confession and hold my breath. Charlie doesn't say anything for a while. I don't press him either, because I understand what I just put out there is a lot to absorb.

Finally, he comes out with this. "I can't believe you still liked me after you saw that buzz cut."

I giggle. Leave it to Charlie to make me laugh at a time like this. To not judge me, but simply to love all that I do and am. Even when I'm admitting to being the world's most unlikely stalker.

"I just wish I'd looked up," he says. "Then I could've been with you this whole time."

He doesn't realize what I've known all along. He's *always* been there with me. "You were," I tell him, then I take a big breath and jump off into the deep end. "I love you, Charlie."

He touches my face. Looks into my eyes. His are filled with tears, but happy ones. "I love you, too."

He pulls me to him and I fall into his kiss. We kiss for every star in the sky. We kiss for every kiss we missed in the past and every kiss we'll miss in the future.

I know my nights are getting numbered. I know my days are getting short. I need to seize every moment I have left. I hang on to Charlie for dear life.

# 24

We're playing cards at my house a few weeks later. I'm definitely more tired, shakier, more fragile than before. The truth is, my grip is so weak I can barely keep my hand hidden from the rest of the players—Charlie, Garver, Morgan, Dad.

And, oh yeah...Dr. Fleming. Or Jessica, as Dad now calls her. It's weird but great.

When she first started checking up on me at home every few days, I felt like I was being a huge burden. I know how busy Dr. Fleming's practice is and how many kids other than me need attending to.

But it quickly became apparent that Dad was starting to look forward to her coming over in more than just a doctor's-patient's-father kind of way. He'd put on his best shirt and shoes, comb his hair just so. I noticed before he did.

"You like her," I finally told him.

"What? I don't know what you're talking about," he replied, a blush creeping onto his cheeks.

"You know exactly what I'm talking about," I said. "And guess what? I approve. So go for it."

Dad somehow found the courage to ask Dr. Fleming— I mean Jessica—out to dinner, and she's been kind of a fixture at our house since then. Dad's super happy he didn't have to take a chance on one of the randos from the dating site. I'm happy I'll be leaving him in good hands. Dr. Fleming has taken great care of me all these years; I'm confident she'll take just as good care of Dad for me once I'm gone.

The terror that once came with thoughts like that is pretty much gone now, too. And it's like the way it was with Zoe—once I let go of the fear, knowing I'm going to die soon has lost its power over me, too. I'm determined to live every second I have left to the fullest for however long that might be. Everything and everyone is going to be okay. I just know it. I wouldn't be able to let go when the time comes otherwise.

Charlie sees me struggling and holds his hand out like a makeshift card holder. I tuck my cards into his palm.

"I'll call," I say with a smile, knowing I'm about to kick everyone's booty with this one.

Morgan reaches across the table and sweeps my chips into the center for me. I flip my cards over from Charlie's hand.

"Full house. Boom. Aces over jacks."

Everybody groans. Jessica shakes her head and throws down her junk hand.

"I had only one pair," she says. "And they were twos! I'm out of chips."

Morgan sweeps the entire pot over to me. "You are officially banned from my casino, Katie."

• • •

The six of us reconvene every couple of nights for the next few weeks. We play cards, watch movies, ask one another questions from my old *Would You Rather...?* book and generally just have a good time. It's awesome to see my dad so relaxed and having someone other than me to hang out with, even though I'm not quite sure what his deal is with Jessica.

And so, one night after everyone's gone home and it's just my dad and me in front of the TV, I get up the courage to ask him. "So, like...are you guys hooking up, or is she friendzoning you?"

My dad gives me a curious look. "I don't even know what language you're speaking, Katie."

I laugh and try again. "I mean, are you guys romantically involved or just friends or what?"

"What," he says.

"You heard me," I tell him, trying to be stern. I really, really want to know. "Your dying daughter deserves an answer."

"And I told you; my answer is what," he says. "As in I don't have an answer yet, Katie. She's just coming off a divorce. I haven't dated in twenty years. So we're taking it slowly. Seeing what happens."

My mouth falls open. "Are you trying to tell me you haven't even kissed her yet? Three weeks of dates and she doesn't even merit a peck good night?"

My dad's cheeks turn light pink. "I'm being a gentleman!"

"Like Nike says, just do it," I tell him, closing my eyes. I'm tired all the time lately. "I like her, Dad. You like her. I want you to be happy. Mom would want you to be happy."

Before I nod off, I hear him say, "You know what? She kind of reminds me of your mom. Maybe you're right."

• • •

A few days later, Morgan, Dad, and I are hanging out watching a baseball game. I'm lying on the couch covered in my favorite blanket, my feet draped over Morgan's legs. My dad sits on the armrest, stroking my hair. Ever since my shakiness got more pronounced and it's gotten hard to swallow, he won't leave my side. He's even set up a blow-up mattress next to my bed in case I need something when I'm sleeping, which is more and more often these days.

During the seventh-inning stretch, Charlie bursts through the door, full of energy.

"Laptop, I need a laptop!" he hoots.

My dad points to the dining room table, where he was working earlier. Charlie pauses to kiss the top of my head, then runs to get it. He plops down on the floor in front of the couch and starts typing.

"Check . . . this . . . out!"

He puts the laptop on the coffee table so we can all see what's gotten him so hyped up. He hits the return key with a flourish. On comes a YouTube video. It's of me, singing "Charlie's Song" at the recording studio.

I have to admit, I sound good. Really, really good. I even look pretty good, too.

Morgan gasps. "Oh my God! What is this? You're amazing, Katie!"

Charlie grins and shrugs. "It's footage from her recording session."

My pulse quickens and I feel brighter, lighter than I have in days.

"You sound incredible," my dad tells me. "You're so beautiful, Katie. You always have been. Inside and out."

I ignore how cheesy that sounds and give him a smile.

"Look at these comments!" Morgan exclaims. "*I'm obsessed with this. I love her voice. She's so hot*—Whoops, sorry, Mr. P."

I am smiling so hard now I feel like my face might explode from happiness.

"Wait, what's that one?" It's the only comment out of, like, a zillion that has a thumbs-down.

"Oh that? That's nothing," Morgan says as she tries to scroll by it. I reach out to stop her.

"I have to get used to critics if my songs are going to be out there for everyone to hear," I say. "I can handle it. Every singer I've ever loved has haters, too."

"Fine," Morgan says with a sigh. "It says *People only like this song because they feel sorry for the dying girl singing it.* Which you know is total bullshit, right, Katie? Sorry for swearing, Mr. P, but it's true."

Despite what I said about wanting to hear the negative feedback, it still feels like a punch in the gut. I wonder if it's true. Are people only listening to my song because they pity me? How would they even know I was a dying girl to begin with?

"Please," Charlie says. "Did you see the screen name of who wrote that?"

I shake my head. Morgan scrolls back to it, then grins and shows it to me. 2LIT4U. I think back to where I've seen it before. Right. Zoe's license plate.

"Ha, that flaming crotch rot just won't give it up, will she?" Morgan crows. "Obviously, you can disregard anything she has to say, Katie. She's just jealous."

"Yeah, and look what else is happening," Charlie says, excitement lighting up his eyes.

He clicks a link on the side and opens a new video. It's a webcam video of a teenage girl playing guitar in her bedroom. She starts strumming, then singing. "Charlie's Song"!

I look at my dad in amazement.

Charlie clicks another link. This is of a different girl reinterpreting the tune from behind a keyboard. Another link. There's a guy sitting on a windowsill singing it a cappella.

"Look at how many people you've touched," Charlie says, an urgency in his voice that I understand all too well. He means *touched before I can't touch anyone anymore.* "Now the whole world can hear you."

I reach out slowly and painfully to him. He grabs my hand and kisses it. He holds it tightly. He won't let go.

"I need to run over to the marina, Katie," he tells me. "But I'll be back in an hour or so."

"I wanna see this Beyoncé-worthy yacht you've been cleaning all summer," Morgan tells him.

"I'm afraid you're gonna miss your chance," Charlie tells her. "Mr. Jones is sailing off on vacation tomorrow. This is my last little checkup before he goes."

"Aw, snap," Morgan says.

Charlie leans down close to me. "I'll see you soon, okay?"

"Sure," I say. He starts to walk to the door, and something in me tells me I should follow. I have a gut feeling that I might not be here when he gets back.

I decide I don't want to just lie here on this couch waiting to die. I want to go on that sunset sail Charlie and I talked about. I want to be in control of how my story ends. "Wait," I say. It comes out forcefully, and everyone turns to look at me. "I want to go with him," I say.

"Go where, sweetie?" my dad asks, concern all over his face.

I struggle to push myself up to a sitting position. "I want to go with Charlie...on the boat. Now." I won't let XP call the shots anymore. It's not over until I say it's over. And I guess what I'm saying is...I'm ready.

It's like everyone in the room freezes. Morgan looks at my dad. I can't tell if she's hoping he'll say yes or no. Charlie stops, waiting for an answer. My dad looks deep in thought.

"Maybe it would be better if you just lie down a little longer," he finally says.

But I'm growing weaker every day, every hour, every minute. Today is my last chance. I know it. I probably won't have a tomorrow even if I don't go.

"It's okay, Dad," I assure him. "I want to."

My father stares back at me, unblinking. I know he

wasn't prepared for this—me making one last stand for independence and freedom. Well, he's just going to have to deal with it.

"I really want to," I insist.

We all know what it means if I go. But I'm okay with it. Really I am. I have to be. There's no other choice.

"Please," I say.

My dad takes a big swallow. Closes his eyes. Finally nods yes.

# 25

Charlie is waiting for me on the boat. I'm standing on the dock with my dad and Morgan, telling her it's okay to cry. She's frantically trying to wipe away her tears. I know she's mad at herself for not being stoic in this moment, but I'm really okay with her showing her true feelings.

Because I feel it, too. I don't want to leave her. She's never left me, not once, even when all the other kids did. I hope she doesn't see my last wish as a betrayal of our friendship.

"Does it hurt?" my dad asks. I'm not sure if he means the sun or his grip around me. But neither does. Not really.

I lower the hood on my sweatshirt and tilt my face up to the sun, holding my arms out wide. The light washes over me. I feel truly at peace. "It feels amazing. It feels better than I even imagined."

I turn to face Morgan. "I love you so much."

She pulls me into a fierce hug. "Everyone sucks compared to you. I'm screwed for life. You've ruined me."

"Well, you saved me," I tell her. "Thanks for not believing Zoe when she said I was a vampire."

Morgan starts laughing through her tears. "That whore? I told you, she is the actual devil. I would never have turned on you."

I shake my head and smile at her. "And you never did."

"And I never will."

"Don't I know it."

I turn to face my dad. I reach out for his hand. I'm staring at him, trying to memorize his face. Every line, every curve, every whisker. I have him to thank for my life. For everything I love and cherish.

"Promise you'll let yourself be happy?"

I can only leave him and get on this boat now if I

know he'll take care of himself after I'm gone. To love and be loved again. Follow his passions to the farthest corners of the earth with someone special by his side, I hope. Maybe Jessica is the one? And if not, someone deserving of the incredible man he is.

Dad nods, his face full of emotion. "I promise."

We hug each other tightly. I want to bottle up everything we've been and done for each other and spread it all over the entire planet. Let the world experience what pure goodness feels like.

"I don't know how the universe works, Katie," my dad says, his voice choked with tears. "But thank you for choosing me to be your dad. I've truly loved every second of it."

I laugh. "I'm not sure that's how it works, but right back at you," I say. "I love you."

"Love you more," my dad tells me.

I shake my head and smile at him. "Not possible."

I turn toward Charlie, who's waiting to help me onto the boat. I wave to my dad and Morgan. "My first boat ride," I say, trying to lighten the moment.

"I'll be right here. On the dock. Waiting for you, okay?" Dad calls out to me.

I nod. "I know you will."

• • •

Charlie has one arm wrapped tightly around me as he steers with the other. He looks gorgeous, strong, in control. He's everything I ever imagined he'd be and more.

My legs buckle under me. I'm so tired. He stares down at me and smiles. "I've got ya. Don't worry."

I gaze out at the horizon, breathing in the beautiful daytime air. Letting myself bask in it. In the sun. It's a mix of colors I've never seen before—a cool blue that fades into purple, which blends into a fiery orange, and all of it is slowly dropping into the edge of the water. It feels like it's just for me. I turn to face Charlie. "I've waited my whole life to feel like this."

He kisses me, and I taste the salt of his tears.

"Me, too," he says.

• • •

"Okay, Katie, time for us to go back in."

I open my eyes and see that my mom is playing her guitar as she says this. The sun is setting behind her, and it's like the sky is on fire. It's the most beautiful thing I've ever seen.

"Can't we stay here forever?" I ask.

"Forever, huh? That's a pretty long time."

"I know," I say, and reach out to strum the guitar along with her.

"Well, let me ask you this: Are you having fun right now?"

I nod.

"Then now is all that matters."

# Epilogue

*Hey, Charlie,*

*I'm sorry I missed you on your way out of town. I must have been out getting supplies for my big trip. Or shots. It's been a while since I've taken a trip where you need shots, and let me tell you, I did not miss that part. Anyhow, I hope Berkeley's treating you well. And as for your note of apology, well, that's just horse shit. It was nobody's fault—and certainly not yours for keeping her out too late that night. I don't want you ever thinking that, and she wouldn't want it either. We knew from when she was young that every day was a gift. Besides, I should thank you. All I ever wanted was for my girl to be happy. You made her very happy, Charlie. And it's nice knowing there's one more person out there who knows how incredible Katie was. One more person out there who loves her.*

*Katie wanted you to have her notebook. She told me to tell you that you stole it so many times, you might as well keep it. She also told me to tell you to read the last page first.*

*Oh! And did you hear Katie's song on the radio? Well, it's your song, I guess. Named for you, anyway. Morgan called me the other day and said she and Garver heard it in the car. My girl, on the radio. Not that I ever doubted she could make it.*

*Take care, Charlie. And don't be a stranger.*

                              *—Jack Price*

*Dear Charlie,*

*I've always been more comfortable writing song lyrics than actual sentences. At least when I'm writing, I can't ramble, no matter how nervous I am.*

*There's no way I can articulate what you've meant to me since that moment we first saw each other. Or the joy you brought me since I first saw you outside my window.*

*You gave me the world.*

*You taught me to live.*

*Even though our time together was short, the stars have been burning for every moment of it. And the light from those moments will be shining down for the next thousand years.*

*I hope that somehow I'll be able to look down and see you, Charlie. To glimpse all of the incredible moments waiting for you. And I hope that you'll occasionally think to look up...and remember all of the light we made together.*

*Amor vincit omnia.*

*I love you, Charlie Reed.*

# About XP

Xeroderma pigmentosum, or XP for short, is an inherited disease that affects only one in a million people in the United States and Europe. (In some other countries and regions of the world, such as Japan and North Africa, it happens more often but is still rare.) People with XP have an extreme sensitivity to ultraviolet rays and get severely burned after just a few minutes in the sun. The DNA damage this causes can't be undone—it just keeps building up over time.

Red and blistered skin, like the sunburns most of us have experienced, are the least of it. Having this rare condition also means having a two-thousand-times higher risk of getting skin cancer. People with XP can also suffer from neurological complications, including loss of eyesight, hearing, and coordination; problems walking, moving, and swallowing; mental confusion; and seizures.

XP is normally diagnosed in early childhood. With extreme vigilance—always staying indoors with all the sunlight blocked out, and wearing protective clothing, sunscreen, sunglasses, and a face shield if going out in the daylight can't be avoided—people with XP can have a normal lifespan. But when these precautions fail, there can be devastating consequences.

In *Midnight Sun*, we've tried to be as realistic as possible in depicting what it's like to live with XP. Still, it's fiction, and for the sake of telling this love story, we've had to take some liberties. For example, it's unclear whether the amount of sun exposure Katie gets from staying out too late with Charlie would have triggered her neurological problems, and her symptoms likely progressed much more quickly than they would in real life.

To learn more about XP, check the following links:

Camp Sundown, https://www.xps.org/camp-sundown
"Camp Sundown: Night Becomes Day," *The Skin Care Foundation Journal*, http://www.skincancer.org/true-stories/night
"The Camp Where the Sun Can't Shine," *Daily Mail*, http://www.dailymail.co.uk/news/article-2732665/The-camp-sun-t-shine-Inside-dark-summer-camp-children-allergic-light.html
"A Family Turns Night into Day for a Child with a Rare Skin Disease," *New York Times*, http://www.nytimes

.com/1997/05/14/nyregion/a-family-turns-night-into
-day-for-a-child-with-a-rare-skin-disease.html

"The Kids Come Out at Night," *Times Union*, http://
www.timesunion.com/local/article/The-kids-come
-out-at-night-4680456.php

National Organization for Rare Disorders, https://
rarediseases.org/rare-diseases/xeroderma
-pigmentosum

The Xeroderma Pigmentosum Society, https://www.xps.org

XP Family Support Group, http://www.xpfamilysupport.org

# About the Author

Trish Cook is the author of six young-adult novels, including *Outward Blonde*, *Notes from the Blender*, and *A Really Awesome Mess*. In her spare time, she's a runner, rower, and wannabe guitarist. She dreams of being on *The Amazing Race*, but the closest she ever came was getting to the final round of casting for *I Survived a Japanese Game Show* (and unfortunately did not survive that last casting cut). You can visit Trish at trishcook.com.